THE
LEVELLER

THE
LEVELLER

JULIA DURANGO

HARPER TEEN

An Imprint of HarperCollinsPublishers

HarperTeen is an imprint of HarperCollins Publishers.

The Leveller
Copyright © 2015 by Julia Durango

Library of Congress Cataloging-in-Publication Data
Durango, Julia.
    The leveller / Julia Durango. — First edition.
        pages   cm
    Summary: "Nixy Bauer, a sixteen-year-old self-made video-game bounty
hunter, gets in over her head when she attempts to rescue a game developer's son
from a virtual trap"— Provided by publisher.
    ISBN 978-0-06-231401-7
    [1. Virtual reality—Fiction.   2. Video games—Fiction.   3. Adventure and
adventurers—Fiction.   4. Science fiction.]   I. Title.
PZ7.D9315Lev   2015   2014034156
[Fic]—dc23   CIP
                    33614080709388   AC

Typography by Torborg Davern
17 18 19 20 21   PC/LSCH   10 9 8 7 6 5 4 3 2 1
❖
First paperback edition, 2017

*For Ryan Durango & Jack Stevenson,
the original Chang & Moose, who inspired this story
and let me steal their game names.
(Love you, hijos.)*

Reality is a sliding door.

—RALPH WALDO EMERSON

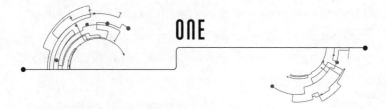

ONE

TYPICAL COOP, I THINK, CLOSING MY EYES AND SINKING INTO THE MEEP.

This'll be the sixth time in six months that Mrs. Cuparino has hired me to drag her sorry son home. Fortunately (or unfortunately, I guess, depending on how you look at it), Dean "Coop" Cuparino, like most of the guys at my high school, is an easy egg to crack. His MEEP world hardly varies from the standard-issue sports-hero template. Today it's football again, Coop's favorite.

My ear trans begins the frequency code and a few seconds later I wake up in the Landing, the MEEP entry zone. A three-story virtual mall of glass and gold, the Landing sparkles like a shopaholic heaven, enticing faithful spenders into the fold. Filled with dozens of flashy boutiques, stores, and salons, here you can purchase character enhancements for your avatar, as well as costumes, weapons, tools . . . anything you might want or need for the world you've created.

I usually skip the shopping spree. First of all, it costs *real* money, and I need every penny I earn to go to my college savings, not pretend makeovers. And second, I like my avatar to look like me, no enhancements; it's one of my personal rules, and I pride myself on it.

To be fair, most people I know design their avatars to look like themselves, at least in basic attributes: hair, skin, eye color. I suppose we all have big enough egos to think we look pretty decent the way we are—just a few minor adjustments away from fabulous. That's where the MEEP enhancements come in. The guys make themselves taller and chiseled, pimple-free with washboard abs. The girls give themselves gorgeous hair, silky skin, white teeth, and Barbie-doll bodies.

I understand the temptation, I really do. But here's what happens. You get used to looking like a million bucks in the MEEP, and then . . . *BAM!* Game over. You're backslapped to reality and wake up with your same old blemishes, bedhead, and ratty sweatpants. All of a sudden you can't *stand* yourself. You've seen what your perfect self looks like in the MEEP, so when you look in the mirror now, all you see are your flaws.

You're just a sad, sorry replica of your pretend self.

My mom calls it the Michael Jackson Effect—never being

happy in your own skin. She warned me about it early on, urging me not to change anything but my costume in the MEEP. Not that I fall for that kind of virtual dream fulfillment anyway. My personal MEEP games involve questing and battle in my own custom-created worlds, not the lame "luvme" templates, like the one I'm in now.

I don't know how these feel-good templates even qualify as *games*, really, but at least they provide me with steady income. It's the luvme gamers like Coop who spend a good chunk of their allowances on timer hacks, so they can stay in the MEEP beyond the preset four-hour maximum. I suppose it's hard to break yourself away from all that *luvin'*. . . .

In any case, I've decided I have to break my own rule about enhancements today. But only because it's a necessity, the price of doing repeat business. Like I said, I've already dragged Coop's butt out of the MEEP five times before. If he sees me coming, he'll run the other way—and fast. I need a disguise, one that Coop will run *toward*.

I quickly start shopping. Time is money. A few minutes later my hair is big and blond, my teeth are white enough to blind a sharpshooter at ten paces, and my boobs are large enough to lift me off the ground and fly me to Oz. Last, I buy a dress roughly the size of a washcloth and matching stilettos that should be classified as lethal weapons.

Oh yeah. Coop is a goner.

I take two steps before I realize I'm wasting valuable time teetering around in these ridiculous anti-walking devices. I slip the heels off and double-time it out of the Landing and through the football stadium toward the players' clubhouse.

The stadium is empty. It doesn't take a PhD to guess what's happened here. The football game is over, probably lasted no more than fifteen minutes. The star quarterback (Coop, naturally) made a string of miraculous plays, handily winning MVP honors, and is now most certainly enjoying the post-game luvme celebration. ("Ladies, come rub against me and smell the swagger!")

I hear the party before I'm halfway across the field. The music is pumping loud and bass-heavy, interspersed with the high-pitched giggles of programmed Meeple.

As I reach the clubhouse door, I put my heels back on and tug the hem of my dress, which has inched its way up to my hips. "Time for the grab and go, Nixy," I tell myself, plastering a vacuous smile on my face. I step inside and immediately let out a huge bark of a laugh, nearly blowing my cover.

The usual bikini-clad babes are all over the place, in and out of the twelve-person hot tub in the middle of the room. But it's not the Meeple making me laugh—Coop always populates his MEEP worlds with big-bosomed, underdressed women—it's Coop himself who's cracking me up. The boy's really outdone himself this time. Not only has he given himself the body of

Arnold Schwarzenegger, but he's squeezed it all into a bright yellow Speedo. Hell, it looks like he's attached a bag of lemons to his pelvis.

Oh, this is going to be good.

I swing my bouncy blond hair and strut my bodacious body over to him. His eyes light up when he sees me and I try not to smirk. For a second I almost feel sorry for the heap of humiliation I'm about to serve him . . . but then I remember what a tremendous jerk he is at school and the flash of guilt dissipates immediately.

"Hey there," I say stupidly, smiling. Coop smiles back and we dazzle each other with our perfect mouthfuls of bleached teeth. (In real life, Coop has an overbite and my bottom teeth are slightly crooked, due to not wearing my retainer on a regular basis.)

"New to the party, babe?" he asks, putting an arm over my shoulder.

I nod enthusiastically and bat my long lashes. "I can't believe I'm here with the MVP!" I squeal. "I'm the luckiest girl ever! You're so amazing!"

He grins smugly and looks down my dress. "Just doing my job, babe, keeping the fans happy."

I lick my lips at him seductively. "And now it's *my* turn to make *you* happy," I purr, pulling him closer.

"Oh yeah?" says Coop, nearly drooling into my cleavage.

"Oh yeah," I whisper. "But first," I add, raising my voice and enunciating clearly into the MEEPosphere, "*I want to see the real you.*"

Coop's face freezes. He knows that MEEP cheat all too well. It's one of my favorites.

"Damn it, Bauer," he growls, pulling away from me as his enhancements disappear.

Now he's just an awkward, normal-size teenage boy: five inches shorter, five inches less around the pecs, and a saggy yellow swimsuit.

I consider getting rid of my own ridiculous enhancements now, but I admit, I enjoy towering over him in my heels. I glance at his Speedo and titter behind a manicured hand.

Coop's face turns red. "You stinking, money-grubbing traitor!" he shouts at me, stalking toward the Landing. He doesn't even try to stall; he knows his game is up. He tried fighting me the first few times, but without going into details . . . let's just say it always ended badly for him.

"A job's a job, Coop, and levelling pays way better than your burger-flipping gig," I say, "which you're *late* for, by the way. Better hustle home and get your hairnet on before Mama Coop goes full-psycho on you."

Coop swears under his breath. "One day I'm going full-psycho on *you*, you dirty MEEP rat."

I shrug and follow him back to the Landing. It certainly

isn't the first time I've been sworn at by a disgruntled gamer. Since I started levelling six months ago, I've been called every name in the book. But hey, I'm good at it, and it beats bagging groceries or washing cars. I charge a flat rate: one hundred bucks a pop. Not bad for an hour or less of work. My business motto is "Nixy Bauer, Home in an Hour." If I don't deliver the goods to parents—meaning, drag their wayward sons and daughters back from the MEEP within the hour—they don't have to pay me. That's why they hire me. I'm fast and I never fail to deliver.

I have my tricks, of course. Both my parents work for the MEEP, or MeaParadisus Inc., as it's officially known, so I've grown up with the game, or at least for the three years it was in development before its world release last year. My dad is a concept artist and my mom writes Meeple script. If you think that sounds glamorous, think again. They're basically lowly peons and poorly paid at that, but they do get full access to the MEEP codes and cheats, which are key to levelling. In fact, my mom even writes a lot of the cheats, the little bits of dialogue that cue certain responses. Like "I want to see the real you," the one I just used on Coop; spoken clearly, those words will immediately turn off primary avatar enhancements. Usually that's all I need to say to ruin a game for someone and force him back home.

Of course, MeaParadisus offers a premium security package, which guarantees twenty-four-hour "Safe Return" by licensed officials, or MEEP-O Men, as we gamers call them. The problem is, by the time you pay for the pricey MEEP ear piercing and matching frequency device, who's got an extra grand left over for the security package? Besides, no one ever thinks *they'll* need bailing out, especially teens, and most parents are clueless.

You can't blame them, though—the parents, I mean. In the past, their kids were at least *conscious* while playing video games, even if they did seem stoned or zombie-like. An irritated mother, for instance, could always get in your face and initiate "crazy-lady meltdown" mode with rather prompt results. (My own mom could teach a master class in it, she's so good.) But once a player's in the MEEP, their body just lies around like a limp rag for up to four hours at a time. You can poke it with a stick and it's still not going to move.

At that point, if you really need your kid back in the real world, you have one of three choices:

1. Suck it up, buy the security package, and call the MEEP-O Men, who will shut down the game externally.
2. Wait it out until your kid gets bored in the MEEP. (Yeah, good luck with that.) Or,
3. Call me and have your kid home within the hour for an easy hundred bucks.

Most parents call me. Then they take the hundred bucks out of their kid's allowance or after-school job, so it's no skin off their nose. Parents love me. The kids? Not so much. Whatever. I'm not in this business to make friends.

I've got two pals, Jackson Mooser and Evan Chan-Gonzalez—user names Chocolate Moose and Changatang—who make sure I don't get messed with at school in exchange for the occasional MEEP cheat. I've also promised never to level them, although they don't use timer hacks very much to begin with. After four hours, the MEEP scripts start to repeat themselves, which gets totally annoying, unless, like Coop, all you want to hear is "Oh, Coop, you're my hero!" over and over and over again. No thank you.

I also refuse to level adults. Way too creepy. I can handle parents who want their kids back, but marital disputes? No way. Those things get ugly fast. Usually it's some poor lady with crying kids attached to her legs like barnacles, whose husband is off feeding his ego in a luvme game. Gross. I saw it a couple of times early on, and quickly made a new rule for myself: I only level players ages thirteen to eighteen, and I only work for parents.

Kids under thirteen aren't allowed to play inside the MEEP anyway. They can buy the external package and build their own world if they want, and many do, but for various reasons, including federal regulations in the US, they're not allowed to have the frequency piercing until their thirteenth birthday. And even then, their parents have to sign a yard-long, small-print waiver that most people never read. Certainly, Mrs. Cuparino didn't read it or she might have thought twice before letting her son have instant access to his own virtual Pleasure Island.

Coop beats me back to the Landing. By the time I wake up in my collapsible lawn chair (I insist on providing my own napping equipment), his mom is already laying into him. Coop glares at me as I fold up my chair and take the pile of twenties Mrs. Cuparino has left on the dresser for me. Like I said, we've been through this before. She knows I'm as good as my word.

I take out my phone and glance at the time. Took me less than fifteen minutes to level Coop this time.

Maybe I should raise my rates.

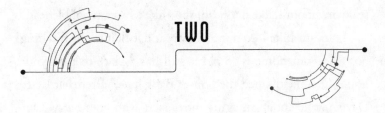

TWO

I RIDE MY OLD SCHWINN HOME WITH THE FOLD-UP LAWN CHAIR strapped to my back and my hoodie tied tightly under my chin. It's mid-November and colder than penguin butt here in central Illinois. I look like a bike-riding Sherpa, but I don't care. I got my driver's license over the summer, but there's no way I'm going to spend money on car insurance, gas, and some old beater in this podunk town. I can get anywhere in twenty minutes or less on my bike, and it's free.

I leave the Cuparinos' north-side subdivision of newer upscale homes, take the side streets to avoid downtown, and finally arrive in my west-side neighborhood of older downscale homes. The houses here are all in ongoing repair, disrepair, or beyond repair. It's the kind of hood where people walk their dogs in their pajamas, nod at you, then flip their cigarette butts in your driveway while their dogs crap on your lawn. My west-side friends and I call it "the ghetto," which makes my Chicago-born mom shake her head. Then again, lots of things make my mom shake her head; she's like a human bobblehead.

I pull my bike into our driveway and lock it to the hitching post. Yes, our home is so old it still has a place to park your horse. Dad nicknamed the house "Baby Jane," after that Bette Davis movie about an aging movie star who goes batty. Our house has had a similar life story. You can tell it was once elegant and grand, the nicest home on the block with its stately Italianate features. Only now the paint has peeled, the porch sags, and the landscaping looks like the victim of a chain-saw massacre.

I enter Baby Jane and stop to give our bulldog, Hodee, a belly rub. Hodee's real name is Don Quixote, which was my mother's bad idea; fortunately, no one calls him that, not even Mom. Hodee's much too tubby and ridiculous-looking to pull off some highbrow literary name, and besides, Hodee likes to keep it real. He lets out a fart while I rub him, then rolls back over and continues to nap.

I follow my nose to a more pleasant aroma in the kitchen, where I smell freshly brewed coffee. Moose and Chang are already there, drinking hot chocolate with whipped cream and chatting up my mom.

"You spoil them, Jill," I say to Mom as I pour myself a big mug of coffee.

"Hello to you, too, Phoenix," my mom answers from the sink, where she's peeling fruit. I know what's coming next: a huge tray of apples and oranges and kiwi, each little bite-size piece stuck through with a colorful toothpick. Every time the guys come over, she insists on serving them a fruit tray, as if they're four-year-olds with scurvy.

Moose wrinkles his nose as I sit next to him with my mug. "Don't be breathing your nasty coffee breath on me, Nix."

I make a face at him and turn to Chang. "Sorry I'm late. I had a job."

"Cuparino?" he asks.

I shrug in response. I like to keep my business confidential. As much as I would love spilling the beans about Coop's Speedo, I never gossip about my marks.

Moose and Chang both smile at my mom as she sets down the preschool fruit tray. Moose pops an orange slice in his mouth, waits for my mom to go back to the sink, then leans in and lowers his voice. "No need to be all zippy-lipped, like you work for the flipping Witness Protection Program. We know it was Coop, we sold him the timer hack this morning."

Chang nods, selecting an apple slice. "You ought to be giving us a kickback," he says in between bites.

I glance at my mom, but she's got her head in the fridge

now, no doubt hoping that dinner will appear if she looks hard enough. "Jeez, you guys, someday you're going to get busted by the wrong parents," I whisper. "Coop's dad is chief of police, you know."

"Relax already, would you? It's not like we're dealing drugs. You think Papa Coop's gonna bust our chops over some video game code?" Moose asks, reaching for another toothpicked orange. "Local PD's got bigger fish to fry than us, Nix."

"Whatever. I just don't want people thinking we're a racket. You do your business, I'll do mine. No discussion, no kick-backs, no nothing. Got it?"

"*Fy fæn*, Nixy, hold the salt, we get it," Chang says. *Fy fæn* is a really bad word in Norwegian that Chang's cousin taught us one summer after his study-abroad program in Oslo. The three of us have used it for years now, since it tends to get us in much less trouble than the English F-word. Our homeroom teacher in sixth grade actually asked us once if "feefon" was the latest slang word for cool or groovy. (We told her it was.) Chang's cousin also taught us the word *rasshøl*, which we use all the time, though not so much around parents and teachers since its meaning is a bit . . . clearer.

"Are we going to play chess now or what?" Chang asks, grabbing two more apple slices, two oranges, and two kiwis. Chang insists on even numbers, even when he's snacking.

"Yeah, let's get this battle going," Moose chimes in, scooting his chair back. "Ma promised to make Tater Tots casserole tonight and I don't want to be late for the love tots."

As usual, we set up the chessboard in the dining room so all the gaming devices in the rest of the house won't distract us. This afternoon it's my turn to play against Chang, while Moose keeps track of our moves in a notebook.

The three of us are on the chess team at school, which has been an ongoing embarrassment. (The chess team, not us.) We have a reputation throughout the region for being the "team most likely to humiliate itself" at every tournament we enter. But I've been elected team captain this year and I intend to turn things around. Not because I actually care about our reputation, but because I need proof of "leadership" for my college applications.

Supposedly, the best universities expect you not only to take part in extracurricular activities (ugh), but also to prove your leadership abilities by "spearheading an exciting initiative" (eye roll). The way I see it, college admissions boards must be made up of former student council try-hards and spirit committee rah-rahs. But I've spent my whole life watching my parents work their butts off for other people, and I am determined not to follow in their footsteps. No fine arts degree for me, no liberal arts education. My goal is to get into the best business school I can, so I can be one of those "other people"—namely, the Boss.

Chess Club was the only extracurricular activity I could stomach. I got Moose and Chang to sign up with me this year and then convince our fellow teammates to vote me in as captain. My sole campaign promise was to provide pizza at every practice, which just goes to show that votes can always be bought for the right price. (Cue Jill Bauer shaking her head again here.)

I'm hoping to improve our team's performance this year, so I can write my college application essays about my "initiative" to make us not suck so bad. Hence, the extra chess practices at my house with Moose and Chang. As it turns out, they're actually pretty killer at the game, maybe due to all the spatial skills they've developed creating custom MEEP worlds. I'm not bad either, although I'm more easily distracted than they are, especially while waiting for my opponent to make his move. By the time it's my turn again, I've forgotten where I am because I've been thinking about a hundred other things.

"Checkmate," says Chang, interrupting my thoughts.

Case in point.

After Chang and Moose shuffle off to their own west-side Baby Janes, I go down to the basement to my dad's studio. Our basement is nothing special—just a big concrete room with exposed beams across the top to hold the rest of the house up—but I love it down here. The walls are lined with homemade bookshelves that are packed full with books, of course, but also loads of art supplies. It smells like oil paint and turpentine, even though Dad hardly ever works on his own art anymore.

A neglected easel sits in one corner with a half-finished painting of a phoenix, my birthday present from two years ago that he keeps promising to work on. Every now and then I cover it with a tarp, not because I don't like it (I do; it's pretty sweet), but because I think it makes Dad feel guilty to look at it every day. He always ends up uncovering it, though. He says it reminds him of what's important.

He's a little sentimental that way. Both my parents are. When they were newlyweds back in the day and still believed in their "dreams"—Mom aspired to be a novelist, Dad a fine artist—they packed their belongings into a little U-Haul truck, grabbed their fresh-off-the-press diplomas from the Art Institute of Chicago, and drove two hours south to this middle-of-nowhere town we now call home.

They rented a small house by the railroad tracks where they could live cheaply and pursue their passions side by side. Sounds so romantic, doesn't it? Only three months in, while they were out buying groceries, faulty wiring in their electric heater started a fire. That blissful love cottage burned to the ground before my parents reached the dairy aisle at Handy Mart.

Everything they had was lost. Mom's novel-in-progress. Dad's paintings. Mom's ancient Apple computer. Dad's art supplies. Every last thing either burned to a crisp or was smoke-damaged beyond repair. The only things left were their old Ford pickup, the clothes on their backs, and two bags of Handy Mart groceries.

That night they stayed at the Motel 6 by the highway. (You see where this is going, right?) Nine months later I was born, and they named me Phoenix Ray Bauer, their "phoenix from the ashes."

I told you they were sentimental.

Dad is asleep on the lumpy couch in the middle of the room, one arm draped over his eyes to keep out the light. An oversize computer monitor sits on the coffee table next to him, casting an eerie screen saver glow over its slumbering slave. Sometimes, I wish I could drape a tarp over it, too.

I tiptoe around the room and start tidying up, gathering coffee mugs and dirty dishes. Dad has obviously pulled another all-nighter. He's in charge of Christmas in the Landing, which will be unveiled on Black Friday—I count on my fingers—only eight days away. Black Friday is also the MEEP's one-year anniversary, so Dad's bosses have told him to pull out all the stops on this. He can't just toss some tinsel around like we do at our house and call it Christmas. Not in the MEEP. This has to be *big*. Dad's been working on it for months.

Mom comes down the basement stairs carrying a dinner tray. I place a hand on Dad's arm to wake him gently, but he startles anyway, popping up like I've blasted a bullhorn in his ear. He looks around and wipes the sleep out of his eyes, then smiles sheepishly at Mom and me. "How are the two most beautiful girls in the world?" he asks as Mom leans down to peck him on the cheek. "Is Christmas over yet? Please say yes."

Mom hands him a big green smoothie. "Afraid not. But no more coffee until you drink this, Vic. And you could use a shower before you get back to work. You smell like a caveman."

"And you look like an extra from *Braveheart*," I chime in. Dad's a big ginger-headed man to begin with, but add several months of beard and hair growth and he looks like some crazy Highlander about to go brawling for fun.

Dad makes a face at us and gulps down the green sludge like a trouper, then reaches for the plate of chicken linguini Mom's made. He pauses in between bites to say, "And what's up with the Nixinator? Been bounty hunting anywhere interesting lately?"

I shake my head. "Same old, same old. Mostly luvme templates with few or no custom elements."

"Filthy casuals," Dad says, winking at me. We both know what's coming next.

Old mama bobblehead starts up. "The MEEP is for everyone, you two, and people have the right to play in it however they like. Besides," Mom adds, unsuccessfully trying to raise one eyebrow at us, "we already have enough hardcore game snobs in the world."

"Never!" I say, but she knows I don't mean it. My dad and I make fun of hardcore gamers as much as we make fun of casuals. As Dad says, we're equal-opportunity teasers.

"So, Nix, got time to try out Christmas in the Landing for me?" Dad asks. "We still have some glitches to fix and a few more mini-games to add, but we're close to the finish line."

"Dinner and homework first," Mom chimes in before I can answer.

"All I have is some pre-calc, which I mostly finished in study hall," I tell her. "And I just ate a ton of fruit, remember? I'll heat up some pasta when I get back, I promise." (Actually, I'd only eaten two kiwi slices and I still have a buttload of homework to do, but what's a little hyperbole between mother and daughter?)

"Great!" says Dad, before Mom can answer. "I'll get it ready to roll."

Mom tries to raise one eyebrow again, but all it does is wrinkle her forehead. Poor Jill. She tries so hard to instill order in the Bauer household, but she is no match for me and Dad.

"Okay," she finally says, "but I want that timer set for two hours max. Got it?" She narrows her eyes at me first, then turns to Dad to make sure he's listening.

"Got it," I say, as Dad nods and types code into the computer.

"Here you go, Nix, two hours," he says, handing me an ear trans.

I plop myself in the comfy old recliner across from the couch and push back until I'm nearly horizontal, then pull a throw blanket over myself. "Nighty-night," I say, clipping the earpiece onto the titanium stud in my left ear. A high-pitched frequency sequence begins to transmit code between Dad's computer and my brain. A few seconds later I'm in the test Landing.

It's the same Landing I was in earlier—the big, glass shopping mall—but now it's on Christmas steroids. Hundreds of thousands of twinkly lights cover every visible surface. A three-story Christmas tree fills the central atrium, its ornaments representing every country on the planet, as well as the one hundred–plus MEEP world templates. A toy plane flies around the tree in spirals, waving a banner behind it that reads PEACE ON EARTH on one side, MEEP ON EARTH on the other.

On a nearby stage a choir of Meeple sing a jazzy version of "Jingle Bells," then segue into "Let It Snow, Let It Snow, Let It Snow" as synchronized fluffy white snowflakes fall from the ceiling. Elves from the fantasy templates stroll through the crowd, passing out sample potions and discount coupons. Every item in every store in the Landing will be "on sale" for the next month, guaranteeing billions of dollars of profit for MeaParadisus Inc.

Not bad for selling the equivalent of the emperor's new clothes—exactly nothing, in other words.

But MEEP shoppers won't care. It's like Diego Salvador, the MEEP's zillionaire founder, says: "They're paying for the *experience.*" And he has a point. Compared with shopping in a real-world mall, the Landing is a cakewalk. First of all, the Meeple walking around are all good-looking and cheery, every single one of them. No whiny tots, no disgruntled husbands, no peevish mothers, no obnoxious tweens. Additionally, no lines, no waiting, no schlepping—your purchases go right into your virtual storage locker.

I spend the next hour checking out all the special features so I can report back to Dad. I visit Santa, who lets me choose a gift from his workshop. (I pick night-vision contact lenses—awesome.) I participate in the gift exchange, where you can donate something from your inventory and get a surprise gift in return. I donate the size-D breast enlargement I'd purchased earlier and happily get an ultra crossbow in return, which I can't wait to try out on my next quest.

I play a bunch of mini-games: Reindeer Racing, Chimney Toss, Snowman Slalom, etc. I kiss Lancelot under the mistletoe at the courtyard King Arthur Yule Party (what can I say, I'm a very thorough beta tester), then check out the *Joyeux Noël* runway show, where all the latest wardrobe options are being modeled. Some of the new medieval dresses are pretty cool and I try some on for fun. One of them actually looks halfway decent on me, so I put it on my Wish List. With my no-curves body and dirty blond hair, I make a pretty convincing wench. Who needs enhancements?

I check the timer and see that I've only got fifteen minutes left, so I head for the main control panel at the Information Desk. MeaParadisus prides itself on "global awareness," so if you're not into the whole Christmas thing, you've got options. I press the HANUKKAH button, and immediately everything's decked out in dreidls and stars of David, the blue-and-white-robed choir belting out Hebrew tunes. I press the rest of the buttons in turn—KWANZAA, WINTER SOLSTICE, BODHI DAY, and so on—and watch the scenery change before me like a fast-forward movie montage.

The final button says HOLIDAY-FREE, which I assume just takes you back to the regular old Landing, but I have two minutes left so I push it anyway. In the blink of an eye, the decorations disappear, the Meeple choir is gone, the party's over. The Landing is blissfully calm and quiet, with only the tranquil burbling of the water fountain to break the silence.

I breathe in and enjoy the low-stim environment after two hours of overload, then jump out of my freaking skin when a huge banner unfurls in front of me. BAH HUMBUG! it says. I barely have time to read it before Santa crashes through the banner in his sleigh and an elfin flash mob starts singing "Grandma Got Run Over by a Reindeer."

At that point I crack up, even though the shock has nearly made me wet my virtual pants.

This little prank has Dad's handiwork all over it. If you

look hard enough, you'll find Vic Bauer's practical jokes hidden all over the MEEP, though they always manage to hit you when you least expect it.

The frequency code summons me back home and my eyelids flutter open. My dad, freshly showered, is on the sofa grinning at me.

I throw a pillow at him and grin back. "Good one, Dad."

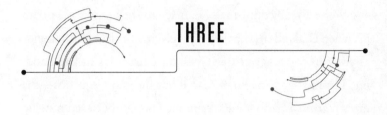

THREE

YESTERDAY, MORE THAN FIFTY MILLION PLAYERS LOGGED ON TO MeaParadisus to shop the Black Friday sales. I think it's safe to say that Diego Salvador is officially richer than the Walmart guy, King Midas, and the pope combined. Mom and Dad are on their second bottle of champagne, having spent most of the day cooking up a belated Thanksgiving dinner now that Dad has emerged from his cave.

Moose and Chang have joined us, making short work of the feast and providing comic relief between obscene mouthfuls of turkey and stuffing. They take turns describing their battles in the MEEP and the custom armies they've created—armored beavers, winged Vikings, amazon samurai—each more absurd than the last.

I've not heard my parents laugh this hard in months. Moose and Chang aren't *that* funny, so my guess is that champagne functions as a humor accelerant; that, or my parents are just extra giddy about having a day off. Either way, it's a good time.

We've already done major damage to the homemade pecan pie when Dad tells us that he's been given $300 in MEEP money as a bonus for his overtime work on Christmas in the Landing. I immediately begin to rant about the grave injustice—the utter *ridiculousness*—of a fake-money bonus, but Dad puts up a hand to stop me.

"Not now, Nix," he says. "Your mother and I have agreed to see only blue skies today."

"But it's grayer than a school mop outside," I protest. "Besides—"

"Zip, zip, zip," Mom says, pretending to thrice zipper her own mouth, though she continues to speak nonetheless. "It's our day of thanks, Phoenix. Tomorrow we can go back to our usual complaints, but today let's just enjoy what we have."

Dad reaches over and tugs my ponytail. "And that means the three of you have three hundred dollars in MEEP money to spend, while Jill and I take a long stroll by the river and pretend it's a gorgeous day in June."

Moose and Chang hoot and bump knuckles at this sudden windfall.

"May your walk be filled with imaginary bluebirds and

daisies, Mr. and Mrs. B," says Chang. "Thanks for all the treats today."

Moose nods in appreciation and rubs his stomach. "Belly full of pie from Mama B, pocket full of MEEP green from Papa B . . . oh yeah, I am *feeling* the Thanksgiving love. You guys are awesome."

I shake my head at my grinning parents. "You guys are *cracked*."

"Indeed," says Dad, bowing to Mom and taking her by the hand as if she's the queen of England. "Cracked as crackers. Now if you'll excuse us, the Premium Saltine and I will be off gallivanting and dreaming of Cheez Whiz for the remainder of the day."

Mom gives us a courtly beauty-pageant wave. "Catch you on the *chip* side!" she calls as they exit the dining room.

Everyone laughs at her joke, even though chips have nothing to do with crackers, and Mom is obviously too tipsy to make the distinction. I laugh too, but make a mental note to hide the third bottle of champagne chilling in the fridge. Someone's got to keep her head in this family.

Half an hour later, Moose, Chang, and I lie sprawled across the living room couch, MEEP devices in front of us, feet propped on the coffee table. While clearing the dining room table and loading the dishwasher, we engaged in some serious debate about how to divvy up the $300 credit. Now we're ready for playtime.

"Once again, to summarize," Chang says, referring to his notebook, "solo battle against skeleton horde, one hundred strong. Two weapons each. Rapunzel's Tower. Thirty minutes. And steer clear of the Black."

I roll my eyes. Lately, Chang's been obsessing about the Black, the empty space that supposedly surrounds the edges of the MEEP world, though I've never seen it, nor has he. Chang insists that the Black is dangerous, that it will fry your brain if you even touch it. I think Chang's been reading too many conspiracy theories—the kind of viral "news" manufactured by bored teens and internet trolls who like to incite hysteria for kicks.

"Yeah, Moose, watch out for Bigfoot too, I hear he'll rip your head off if you even make eye contact," I say, nudging him with my elbow.

"Whatever," says Moose, "I just want to know what my reward is when I beat the pants off you two scrubs."

"Winner gets the last piece of pie," replies Chang, ignoring my previous snark. "Losers scrub the pots and pans."

Moose and I murmur our agreement as we fiddle with our device settings.

"Begin weapons draft. Nixy goes first," continues Chang, like he's initiating countdown on a nuclear deployment.

"Ultra crossbow," I say, eager to test my Christmas exchange gift in timed battle.

"Optic boomerang," says Moose, pretending to fling one through the living room. "Gonna take the crack-a-lacking heads right off those boneheads, CR-ACK, CR-ACK, till they cry wee wee wee all the way home!"

"Explosive slingshot," says Chang, oblivious to Moose's theatrics.

"Mage staff," I continue, selecting it from my inventory.

"Double wrist daggers," says Moose, slicing his hands through the air like a juiced-up ninja. "Gonna slice 'em to pieces, leave a pile of bones in my wake. Hope you suckers got your dish gloves ready."

"Samurai kanabo," intones Chang. "Ready in five, four, three . . ."

We each adjust our ear trans and when Chang says, "Go!" we clip them to our studs.

When I wake up, I run right through the Landing and out the door to Rapunzel's Tower. I've already equipped myself via the external settings on my device so I don't waste time going through my inventory now. Time is precious if I want to win, and I *always* want to win. I may not be a trash-talker like Moose or possess Chang's precision mind, but I have my own strategy that serves me well in the gaming world. On the outside, I play it casual, let the competition think I'm an easy mark, the first man down in battle. On the inside, I'm a machine.

As I book it to Rapunzel's Tower, I hear the skeleton horde screaming their battle cries in the distance, though I can't see them yet. The tower's nothing but a tall, skinny stone turret, just like from the pages of a fairy tale, a popular choice for the timed battles we play.

We invented these mini-games after we got our MEEP piercings a year ago. Since the MEEP only offers a single-player option, there's no way for us to play together, like we did in the nonvirtual game platforms. They say a multiplayer MEEP is in the works, but due to various liability issues with the neuroscience involved, it'll be another year or two before its release. For now, "crisscrossing," or playing across worlds, is a straight-up no-no except for licensed beta testers like me. And even I have to be careful about not abusing my beta code, or the MEEP admins will toss me out of the chowder like a bad clam.

Our mini-game rules, strictly enforced by Chang, go like this. First, we agree upon the constants: same setting, same enemy, same length of time, same number of weapons. Then we run a draft pick for the weapons—no overlap allowed, since they're the variables in the equation. Next, we place our wagers—losers pay for chili dogs at the Pound, winner gets to set rules for the next game, things like that—to stoke the competition. Finally, we battle, each in our own MEEP worlds. After the allotted time, we come back together and compare notes. Whoever destroys the most enemies before dying (or if you're lucky, before time's up) wins.

Afterward Chang writes up the results in his game log to share with LEGION, his online MEEP Geek community. Those guys are all about the data and figuring out how to use it to hack the MEEP. They're probably responsible for the Black rumors too. According to LEGION, Diego Salvador is the Russian czar of the gaming world, and they are the rural peasants, trying to topple the empire brick by virtual brick.

Moose, on the other hand, couldn't care less about stats, efficiency ratios, or how to exploit glitches; he plays solely for bragging rights. And me? I love the rush it gives me, kind of like a runner's high, I suppose—that moment when I feel invincible, like there's no one I can't level.

At *this* moment, however, I'm far from *that* moment. The skeleton horde is now visible on the horizon, charging at me like a sea of rattling bones. I scoot inside and seal the door, then take the stairs two at a time until I'm at the top of the tower, where waist-high stone walls offer me protection on all sides. Even though you can't physically feel pain in the MEEP, your brain still registers all the emotions that go with imminent bodily danger: fear, anxiety, panic, and sometimes even exhilaration, as crazy as it sounds, especially if you have a bit of a masochist streak like Chang. Though certain enemies still freak me out—I've never been overly fond of anything that may want to take a bite out of me, for example—I've logged so many hours in battle and "died" so many times that any dread I used to feel has mostly been replaced by anticipation. Right now I feel jittery, like my palms would be sweating and my heart racing in the real world, but pumped, too, for the fight to come.

I ready my crossbow and wait for the horde to come within range. As they near, I see that they're all dressed in ragtag fashion, like they've just popped into the Goodwill store on the way over. Some wear Civil War uniforms, others jaunty pirate hats and pantaloons; a few sport bridal gowns complete with flowered veils. Apparently, no regulation uniform is required in this oddball regiment. I like it. Even better, their weapons are all handheld: swords, clubs, and axes. Nothing projectile.

"Fish in a barrel," I murmur under my breath, then *whoosh*, I loose my first arrow. A skeleton in a red fuzzy bathrobe goes down like . . . well, like bones in a bathrobe.

"One down, ninety-nine to go," I say, pleased with myself, then quickly take down two more. My ultra crossbow is wicked fast, the perfect weapon at this height. The ragamuffin skeletons skitter around the tower, clamoring to get in. I pick them off right and left, my body working in perfect rhythm as I slide the arrows from my quiver, load, aim, fire.

I can taste the pecan pie now.

Even if Chang's slingshot and Moose's boomerang prove as

deadly as my crossbow, I know I've got better aim than both of them. The rush sweeps over me: I'm in the zone. "Nixy B. for the win," I crow aloud. Right then, a skeleton wearing what looks like a toddler's sailor cap turns to the bonehead next to him and rips the guy's arm right out of its socket.

"Holy sh—" I start to yelp, but before I can finish the obscenity, Sailor Cap flings the dismembered arm bones at me. I duck, but it's too late, the arm too long. The bones hit me right between the eyes and knock me on my butt.

"That was *humerus*," I joke to nobody as I stumble back onto my feet.

Though vexed the horde won't be dispatched as neatly as I'd hoped, I can't help but give a mental high five to the MEEP designer who programmed a big dollop of sassy into these skeletons.

I look down and laugh-snort at what I see next. The horde is working together to form a human—or undead, I should say—ladder up the side of the tower; all that's missing is the circus music and peanuts. They stand on each other's shoulders, three skeletons high on all sides, circling the tower like an overzealous cheer squad. They put our own high school cheerleaders to shame. Mindy and her crew always act a little too cool for school, if you know what I mean. In contrast, these boneheads have spirit, yes they do!

The spryer skeletons are now climbing the ladder, cracking

their comrades' bones with impunity as they use a rib cage here, a skull there, for purchase. I manage to ward off the first wave with some quick-fire crossbow action, but there are too many, too fast.

I whip my mage staff from the holster on my back and crouch down, tensely waiting for the second wave. One exhale is all I get before they come scrabbling over the stone walls like clicking white spiders. I jump to my feet and pivot-spin a full 360, taking off four skulls with my outstretched staff—*WHACK, WHACK, WHACK, WHACK.*

Not bad, I think, stopping to catch my breath before the third wave arrives.

CLICK CLICK, I hear behind me. My heart races as I twirl around, staff at the ready.

I'm face-to-face with my old pal, Sailor Cap, who clacks his big grinning teeth at me, then plunges his sword through my heart. Though I feel no pain, the force knocks me backward, and I drop my mage staff.

Fy fæn.

Score one for the boneheads.

As I slump to the stone floor, my ear trans starts beeping at me, summoning me back to real life. I can't believe thirty minutes have passed so quickly—I would have guessed no more than fifteen—but then again, it's easy to lose track of time in battle.

When I open my eyes, my parents hover over me, staring into my face. I nearly jump out of my skin. "Jeez!" I yell, sitting up on the couch. "That's totally creepy! What are you *doing*?"

My parents look at each other, like they're trying to decide which one of them should answer. As I try to back away from their looming faces, I notice that Chang and Moose are still asleep on either side of me.

"Did you guys override my ear trans?" I ask, irritated by the parental intrusion. This really isn't their style. "And why are you back already?"

Mom clears her throat. "Phoenix, our boss just called—"

Uh-oh, I think. *Too much unauthorized bounty hunting. They're shutting me down.* "Little boss or big boss?" I ask, turning to my dad.

"*The* boss," he says. "Very very big big boss."

"Diego *Salvador* called?" I ask. My mind is whirling. Surely the MEEP's head honcho doesn't deal with small-fry levellers like me. That's what minions are for. "So what did he want? Are you both getting huge promotions?" I ask and fake a smile, though I know that's definitely not the case. My parents look way too serious for this to be good news.

Mom shakes her head. "It's his son . . . Mr. Salvador's only son has gone missing in the MEEP."

So I'm not busted. I shrug as the relief washes over me. "Tell them to send in the MEEP-O Men," I say. "Kid's probably hiding out in some virtual tiki hut surrounded by topless hula dancers. They'll find him soon enough."

Dad frowns. "It's not that simple, Nix. Apparently they've been trying to reach Wyn for days, but he's managed to barricade himself in."

"Well, that was asinine," I say. "But he'll surface soon. His real body's gotta be pretty hungry by now."

My parents exchange a grim look.

"That's just it, sweetie," says Mom. She takes my hands and kneels beside me. "He left behind a suicide note."

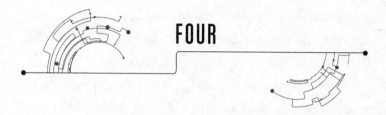

FOUR

DIEGO SALVADOR'S PRIVATE JET IS SO SWANK I KEEP REACHING INTO my pocket for my phone. I'm dying to take a photo of myself reclining in the leather lounge chair, sipping ginger ale from a crystal glass, so Chang and Moose can see what they're missing. But then I remember that this is all supposed to be TOP SECRET, like we're on some James Bond spy mission to Russia. All that's missing is an exotic-looking woman with a bountiful rack named Anita Shelferdeez and we'll be set.

Unfortunately, I'm not able to share these thoughts with anyone else on this fancy tin can because I'm surrounded by furrowed brows: Dad, who's next to me, squinting into his laptop, and Kora Lee, who's across from us, grimacing at her phone. Kora is Diego Salvador's personal assistant, sent to collect us at the heinous hour of six this morning at the small airfield outside of town.

After my parents broke the news to me yesterday about Salvador's missing son, things went a little crazy. Chang and Moose were shuffled out the door with Tupperwared leftovers, my mom answering their puzzled faces with nondescript murmurs: "Family emergency, nothing to worry about, Great-Aunt Martha . . ."

Once they were gone, Dad dialed up Diego Salvador on his laptop, while I combed my fingers through my hair and grumbled a bit. Here we were, about to videoconference with the richest, most powerful man on the planet, and I was wearing an old Zelda T-shirt with a fresh gravy stain on the chest.

I don't think Mr. Salvador noticed. When his face popped on the screen, it looked just like it had on the cover of *Time* magazine last year when he was declared Man of the Year: tan, handsome, slightly graying hair, a jaw that meant business. He greeted us tersely, managing a polite nod of the head for my mom, but clearly in no mood for small talk.

"Phoenix," he said, turning his attention to me.

I grabbed Hodee, who was curled up underneath my feet, and tried to cover the gravy stain with him.

"Your parents tell me you're quite a creative beta player," he continued.

I shrugged, unsure of what to say. Did he know about the levelling? That could be bad.

"In fact, they say you have a talent for finding players in MeaParadisus, whether they want to be found or not."

Yup. He knew. I glanced at Jill then and she nodded slightly, which I took to mean: *The jig is up; go ahead and speak freely.*

I cleared my throat. "Well, I don't know that I can find *anybody*, but I haven't failed yet. I'm pretty familiar with the various MEEP templates, which helps."

"Yes, my usage admin shared your stats with me. You've spent nearly as much time in the MEEP as my full-time developers . . . lots of late-night hours you've racked up over the past year."

At that point, both my parents whipped their heads around to look at me. I kept my gaze on the laptop screen and avoided all eye contact with them, glaring instead at Salvador. How many ways could I be ratted out in one day? First, my parents tattle on my levelling business, then Salvador tattles on my nighttime usage? Did personal privacy mean nothing anymore?

"I'd like your help, Phoenix, on a very challenging retrieval mission," Salvador continued, completely unfazed by my I-can't-believe-you-people gaze. "May I count on you?" he asked.

"How much does it pay?" I replied without blinking. Jill gave a little gasp beside me while Vic did a slow-motion face palm. I'd obviously just embarrassed the hot heck out of them, but I figured it was time for payback in that department.

Diego Salvador's eyebrows raised the slightest fraction of a millimeter, but otherwise he matched my poker face steel for steel. "Interesting question. I suppose I should ask how much you charge your other clients when you engage in levelling . . . in direct violation of the beta agreement, may I add."

I opened my mouth to defend myself, but Salvador put up a hand to stop me. "No need to worry, Phoenix. As I told your parents earlier, I understand that all business enterprises of a grand scope like MeaParadisus will naturally produce an intrepid subclass of entrepreneurs such as yourself. Which is exactly the kind of guts and initiative I need. Will five thousand dollars plus expenses suffice?"

I pretended to think this over while my mother gave me a swift kick underneath videocamera range. Ah, maternal love. "Fine, but I'd like a five-K bonus if I get him back in an hour," I said. *What the heck?* I figured. *He's a billionaire; ten thousand dollars is chump change to him. I have college tuition to think about.*

"Done," he said. "I'll send my plane for you first thing in the morning. I prefer to discuss the details in person."

So that's how Vic and I ended up here, swigging ginger ale and winging our way to Salvador's place in the Florida Keys. After some discussion, it was decided that Dad would accompany me for tech support, while Mom and Hodee would stay home and hold down the fort. Of course, then Jill had to give me the whole eight-hours-of-sleep lecture and threaten to lock down my MEEP device at night if I couldn't control myself in the future. To be fair, though, she was a champ this morning, getting up at five o'clock to make coffee and drive us to the airfield.

A little bell dings in the plane, and Kora, who's said very little to us so far except to take our drink orders, unbuckles herself from her seat and leans forward. "Mr. Salvador has instructed me to fill you in on some of the details before we arrive, to save time once we get there," she says, removing a digital tablet from an expensive-looking leather briefcase.

Kora Lee is dressed in a white silk blouse, a red pencil skirt, and black pointy heels that say "sexy" and "don't even think about it" at the same time. Her long black hair is parted perfectly down the middle, her makeup so immaculate she almost looks airbrushed. I wonder how she does it, how she achieves this perfection, given that she and the pilot left Florida in the middle of the night to arrive in Illinois by six. I suppose when your boss is Man of the Year, there's no such thing as "weekend casual" or flying in your jammy pants.

"Three days ago, while his father was in California to launch Christmas in the MEEP," Kora begins, in the precise, clipped voice of a newscaster, "Wyn Salvador entered a custom MEEP world of his own creation. Later that day, when his grandmother, Betina Oviedo, or Mama Beti as she is called, summoned him for Thanksgiving dinner, he was still in a state of MEEP sleep. Though surprised her grandson would skip a holiday dinner, Mama Beti was accustomed to Wyn spending much of his time in the MEEP, so she had no cause for alarm at that point. She had a dinner tray sent to his bedroom in case he woke up hungry, then she herself went to bed."

My dad and I exchange a guilty glance. We've both done the exact same thing before—gamed through dinner, only to wake up later and find a sandwich next to us with an attached note from Jill saying "Eat this, knucklehead." It's easy to lose time in the MEEP, especially if you aren't hampered by the automatic shutoff.

Kora continues. "When Mama Beti went to check on him the next morning, Wyn was still MEEP sleeping, his ear trans still active, his food cold and untouched. She immediately called her son in California. Mr. Salvador dispatched a programmer to enter Wyn's MEEP world and bring his son back."

I nod and throw back a little more ginger ale. So far this is the same story I've heard a hundred times before, ever since I started levelling: kid escapes to fantasy world until his parents get fed up and drag him back to reality. Although given that Wyn's dad is a flipping billionaire, how bad can Wyn's reality be, I wonder. A mansion in Key West, servants, private plane? I shake my head. Rich kids, so spoiled.

"The programmer made it to the Landing with no problem," says Kora, "but trouble began as soon as he entered Wyn's custom MEEP, a maze of sorts."

My ears perk up. "A maze?" I ask.

"Yes. It seems Wyn built a series of rooms and corridors, a labyrinth, outside the Landing. Each room presents a different challenge to the player."

My dad and I exchange another glance, eyebrows raised, a glint in our eyes. I know he's thinking the same thing I am: sounds like fun. But then just as quickly, Dad's face transforms back to Serious-Father look. "So where does the suicide note come into play, Miss Lee?" he asks, reminding me that I mustn't appear too jaunty on this trip.

"It's not a suicide note per se, rather a message contained in the first room. According to the various programmers who've entered—there have been several in the past few days—the room is completely white. Once you step into the center of the room, words appear on the walls. Here, I'll read them to you."

While Kora scrolls down on her tablet, my dad and I lean forward, eager to hear the first piece of the puzzle.

"Now begins the great adventure," Kora reads. "Though I leave behind a body, my soul will live forever in the MEEP."

Oh for the love of God and sprinkled donuts. What a drama queen. I try not to roll my eyes, but I obviously don't succeed because my dad frowns back at me. "*My soul will live forever in the MEEP?*" I repeat. "Didn't anyone explain to him that the MEEP is a *game*, not an afterlife?"

"Ease up, Nixy, it's not for us to judge his thoughts or beliefs,"

Dad says. "Clearly, he was—*is*—a distraught young man."

I shrug, but let it go. Wyn's message doesn't sound very distraught to me; more like some eager cult member who just drank the MEEP Kool-Aid.

"So what happens after that?" I ask Kora. "After the message appears?"

Kora hesitates and furrows her flawless brow. "The floor opens and drops you into a shark tank."

My heart stops for a moment. "*Fy fæn*," I mutter under my breath. A shark tank? What kind of a sadistic *rasshøl was* Wyn Salvador? Like I said, even though you can't feel pain in the MEEP, you can still feel terror and horror and paralyzing fear. And sharks happen to be my *worst* fear, which is why I'm perfectly happy living in Illinois: plenty of land mass between me and those beady-eyed eating machines.

"That's just evil," I say with a shiver, really feeling for the programmer who first made the awful discovery. I'd rather be burned to a crisp by a fire-breathing dragon—and I *have*—than be the next victim of *Jaws*'s toothy shredder.

My dad is frowning big-time now. He knows how I feel about sharks. "So Wyn was allowed access to all the in-house prototypes?" asks Dad, with more than a hint of anger in his voice. "A shark tank would be impossible to create with the currently released modules."

"Mr. Salvador gives his son full access to the database," Kora replies in her clipped voice. "Wyn likes to experiment with the newer modules and he provides valuable feedback. His father trusts him implicitly."

"Sounds like that was a mistake," grumbles Dad.

Kora purses her lips. "I believe your daughter has access to some beta modules as well?"

"Yes, but she doesn't abuse it," says Dad, which is technically not true, but I do my best to play the part and look innocent.

Kora casts a skeptical eye in my direction, then nods curtly at Dad and continues to scroll through her tablet.

"What happens after the sharks?" I ask, after a moment of awkward silence.

"Anaconda," Kora says matter-of-factly and, unless I am imagining it, with a bit of pleasure at my expense.

"Nice," I murmur.

"I believe there are carnivorous plants in that room as well," she adds.

"Wow, this Wyn sounds like a real nature lover," I say, feeling myself loathe the guy more and more with each passing moment.

"The programmers who've entered the maze have made a diagram of their findings," Kora says, pressing an icon on her tablet and passing it to me. "You should use the rest of the flight to familiarize yourself with it."

I take the tablet from her and Dad leans in to look over my

shoulder. After a few moments, he lets out a long whistle. "Looks like Wyn thought of everything, didn't he?" he asks.

"And this may just be the beginning," Kora replies.

I look at her in question.

"None of the programmers made it to the end of the maze," she explains. "No one made it past the fourth room."

"So what, they just quit? Or are they still working on it?" I ask.

Kora turns her eyes from me. "As of yet, none of them wish to reenter the maze. Some of them are physically exhausted and are recuperating in one of Mr. Salvador's medical facilities. Others are . . . compromised."

"Compromised?" my dad asks, frowning again at Kora.

Kora shifts uncomfortably in her leather seat. "The doctors think perhaps a slight case of PTSD, though that has yet to be verified."

"They went crazy?" I ask, my voice louder than I mean it to be, while Vic snorts at Kora's soft-pedal.

"Perhaps it's more accurate to say they went into shock," replies Kora. "In any case, they're all currently under the care and supervision of the world's best doctors. I'm sure they will be fine after a short rest."

"And you expect me to send my only daughter into some monstrous playground that scared the living daylights out of grown men?" Dad asks.

Kora bristles. "Not all the programmers were men, Mr. Bauer."

Now it's Dad's turn to shift uncomfortably and I can't help it—I grin behind my hand. I mean, Kora does have a point, even if she's using it to change the subject.

"My apologies," Dad says, then clears his throat. "I didn't mean to imply, of course, that—"

"But back to the maze," I say, trying to save my dad from any more potential embarrassment. "So no one knows how it ends. And we can only assume that Wyn saved his best defense for last."

Kora nods.

"The Big Bad," my dad mutters. "God only knows what that might be."

I blow a long breath out of my cheeks.

If there's something worse than a shark tank, I'm not sure I want to know.

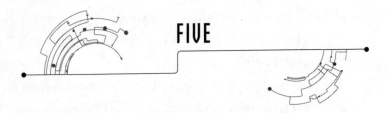

FIVE

I LOOK OUT THE WINDOW AND SEE THE PERFECT BLUE GULF OF MEXICO below me, the Florida Keys stretched out like a long tentacle through the sea. I try to breathe in the beauty of it, but the tentacle has reminded me of a giant squid and now it's all I can think about. Giant squid. Could *that* be Wyn's grand finale?

God, I hope not.

After going through the list of maze obstacles with my dad, I'm not sure whether I want to congratulate Wyn after I level him, or break his nose. He certainly chose some creative ways to keep people from finding him.

"Looks like he's preying on people's phobias," my dad says as we study the diagram together in awe and horror.

Claustrophobia, arachnophobia, agoraphobia . . . Wyn

tucked them all into his little shop of horrors, almost as if he'd had a pile of mental health brochures by his side to use as a blueprint. No wonder some of the programmers cracked trying to rescue him.

The plane begins to descend and Kora directs our attention to one of the islands near the tip of the chain. "That's Abigail Key, the Salvador estate."

"They have their own island?" I ask. "I thought they lived in Key West. I saw a picture of their mansion in *Time* magazine last year."

Kora nods. "You're thinking of Casa del Sol. They own that, too. Mr. Salvador conducts most of his business from the Casa and entertains there as well. That's where my own office is located, in fact. But he prefers to keep Abigail Key private, for family use only."

"Abigail was the name of Diego's late wife," Dad explains. "Abigail Brooks. She was a world-class pianist. Passed away a few years ago."

I vaguely remember this from the magazine article. Some kind of rare bone cancer, I think.

"The island estate was Diego's gift to her," Kora says. "It's where the family retreated when she became ill."

I peer down at the island, a lush green paradise growing right out of the sea. A runway cuts through the trees along the eastern shore. On the opposite side I spy the top of a sprawling mansion with a crystal-blue pool winding along the back of it like a river. I can also make out a pair of tennis courts, a boat house, and a dock with several boats anchored to it, including a small yacht. An incredulous snort escapes from my nose or mouth or wherever snorts primarily originate. Abigail Key looks just like the fantasy island template in the MEEP, only it's the real thing.

This is what Wyn Salvador is running from? His own private paradise?

A few minutes later we taxi down the runway and soon we're released into the hot island air. I feel my hair immediately frizz in the humidity while my black T-shirt and jeans cling to me like foil on a baked potato. So this is why people wear white in the tropics. A crisply dressed chauffeur (in white, as if to prove my point) shuttles us from the runway to the house in the queen mother of all golf carts, with gold-stitched leather seats, a small refrigerator (we may help ourselves to its contents, says the chauffeur), and even a rooftop air conditioner, which blows a cool mist onto my neck. Suddenly I feel like I'm in Disneyland, only I forgot my tiara and princess dress. Right now I look closer to someone's rotten stepsister with my big rebellious hair and melting mascara.

Kora leads us into the mansion and I try to act cool, like I'm not completely agog at the palatial furnishings, the artwork, the total dripping-in-wealth feel of the place. We go up a grand staircase, down a hall, and into what Kora calls the conservatory, like we're playing a big game of Clue. The vast room is all skylights, blossoming plants, fresh-cut flowers, and wicker furniture scattered about. An ivory-colored grand piano sits in the middle of the room, though its keyboard is closed, its embroidered bench tucked up beneath it like a foal snuggling its mother. I draw closer to look at the framed photograph ensconced between two vases of small pink roses on top of the piano. A pretty woman with light brown hair and kind green eyes smiles out from the photo.

"That's my Abigail," a voice says, and I turn around to see Diego Salvador walk in. "This was her favorite room in the house."

"I can see why," says Dad, walking over to shake hands with his boss. Though Dad has cleaned up well for the occasion, shaved the Neanderthal beard and trimmed his hair, he still looks like he belongs in a grassy field hefting boulders and throwing hammers for fun. In contrast, Diego Salvador, though almost as tall as Dad, has the lean, muscular look of a soccer player or distance runner. The thought flickers through my mind that they would make an interesting match for each other on the battlefield. Dad would have extra strength and heft on his side but Salvador looks a little lighter on his feet, and faster perhaps.

"Isn't that right, Nixy?" Dad says, and I realize I've spaced out and missed part of the conversation. Dang. I nod and agree with who-knows-what, then smile at everyone, trying to cover for my brain lapse but pretty sure I just look like an idiot. Not a great way to start the job.

A young man clad in the same white servant uniform as the chauffeur rolls in a cart of coffee, orange juice, and individual quiches, and Salvador leads us to a small seating arrangement set in an alcove of floor-to-ceiling windows overlooking the sea.

My dad and I dig into the quiches while Salvador and Kora look on.

"Please excuse me if I seem rushed," Salvador says, signaling the servant to pour us some coffee, "but I'm sure you understand my urgency."

"Of course," Dad says, putting down his fork. "Three days your son has been in MEEP sleep now?"

Salvador nods. "Four, counting today. We have a doctor monitoring his vital signs and feeding him intravenously." He looks at me now. "You've studied the diagram, I presume?"

I swallow the last bite of a very tasty bacon-and-cheese quiche so I can speak. "I have. Your son seems quite determined to be left alone, given the amount of traps and torments he left behind."

Salvador's face darkens. "Yes. I take full responsibility for that. I should have been here for him. Thanksgiving was Abigail's favorite holiday. I never missed it when she was alive, but since her death, I've always arranged to be away. I should have realized it would be a hard time for Wyn, too."

I don't know what to say. Thankfully, Dad clears his throat and comes to the rescue. "Parenting is a tricky job, especially where teenagers are involved," he says, his eyes flicking my way ever so slightly. "They sometimes act rashly, say or do provocative things, because they want our attention."

I beg to differ but I keep my mouth shut.

"Let's just do our best to get Wyn out of there," Dad continues, "and then I'm sure the two of you, father and son, will get things sorted out."

Salvador nods. "Of course. Let's get started, then. Are you up for the challenge, Phoenix?"

I pause for a second and Dad jumps in again. "Look, Mr. Salvador—"

"Please, call me Diego."

"Diego, before we send Nixy or anyone else into a very frightening situation, I've been wondering . . . why not try the Reset button on the Landing console? A reset would restore the game to its default settings and Wyn would automatically be released from the MEEP."

Salvador shakes his head impatiently. "We've thought of that, of course. But Wyn himself would need to be in the Landing for that to work. The game won't reset if a player is still at large."

"Right," says Dad, rubbing his jaw. "Then how about shutting down the entire MEEP for a bit, activating a mass Awaken frequency?" he continues. "I realize you'd get complaints by the thousands, but the world can survive without a game for a few minutes."

Salvador frowns. "Too risky, I'm afraid."

"Risky how?" I ask. I've been wondering the same thing myself. Kora had already explained that the MEEP-O Men had been unable to shut off Wyn's game externally, that none of their usual Awaken codes had worked. But surely Diego Salvador had the power to reset the whole game. "You activate the frequency, everyone wakes up. . . . What's at risk besides a few million grumpy players who've had their game interrupted?"

"It's not that simple, Nixy," Kora says, glancing at Salvador for permission to go on. He nods at her, and I sense some impatience in his eyes. He clearly wishes to be done with this conversation.

"Everyone playing on a regulation frequency would wake up, yes," explains Kora, "but we're not sure what would happen to players who've used nonregulation codes to enter."

"Hackers, you mean?" asks Dad.

"Yes, there is some . . ." Kora begins, then pauses to search for a word, "*speculation* that a mass Awaken frequency would leave any nonreg players in a kind of limbo."

Dad and I both raise our eyebrows at that.

"Limbo?" Dad says, turning to Salvador.

Salvador drums his fingers on the arm of his chair. "Possibly comatose," he finally says.

"Comatose?" I repeat, slamming my orange juice down harder than I mean to. I run a finger down the edge of my left ear and feel the small metal stud there. "What about all the safeguards you guys are supposed to have in place? All that medical research done to make sure the MEEP doesn't fry our brains?"

"The MEEP is perfectly safe for those who abide by the contract," Salvador assures us. "However, we cannot guarantee the safety of *intruders* or those who choose to bypass the safeguards."

My stomach turns upside down. I think of Chang and Moose, who constantly experiment with nonreg frequencies. They're probably in the MEEP right now using one of their hacks.

"So Wyn must have used a nonreg code to bypass the timer?" Dad asks.

"Yes," Salvador says. "So you see why I hesitate to activate a mass Awaken. Many lives might be at stake, including my son's. Believe me, we've explored every angle. Your daughter is our last attempt at in-game retrieval. If Phoenix fails, however, I'll take the risk and shut down the MEEP. I already have the best doctors in the world on call if that becomes necessary. I want my son back."

"And what about everyone else?" I say. "The people who

don't have fancy doctors on hand and billions of dollars to pay hospital bills?"

Salvador shrugs. "I save my concern for those who play by the rules, Miss Bauer."

So it's *Miss Bauer* now. Apparently I've ticked him off. "I'll be sure to pass that on to your rule-abiding son when I find him," I say. "And I *will* find him. Just don't turn off the MEEP."

"Very well," he says, rising to his feet. "Shall we?"

As we follow him out of the room, I feel my phone vibrate in my jeans pocket. My phone! I've got to call Chang and Moose *now*.

"Excuse me, I need to use the restroom first," I say.

Salvador looks me up and down. I swear his eyes linger on the pocket where my phone is.

"Long flight, gallons of ginger ale," I explain with a quick laugh, hoping I merely sound stupid instead of nervous.

Salvador narrows his eyes at me and we stare at each other for a bit. Finally, he nods at Kora. "Please show her to the guest facilities," he says, then turns to me. "I'm sure I need not remind you of our privacy agreement."

I give him my best poker face. "I'm a vault, Mr. Salvador."

I follow Kora down the hall and she gestures to a door. "When you're finished, you can meet us in Wyn's room. Go back the way we came, past the conservatory, last door on your right."

"Got it," I say, then lock myself in the bathroom. It is, of course, bigger than my bedroom at home. I sit on a sofa-type lounge chair—do people really need to rest after using the toilet?—and dial Chang; Moose never keeps his phone charged, and besides, he's usually with Chang anyway.

"Nixy," Chang answers in his flat voice.

"Put Moose on speaker phone," I tell him, keeping my voice as low as possible, and wait until I hear Moose's signature greeting in the background.

"How's tricks, Nix?" he mumbles through what sounds like a mouthful of something. Peanut butter Pop-Tart, if I know Moose.

"Listen," I say. "I'm on a job and don't have much time. You guys need to stay off any and all nonreg frequencies until you hear back from me. Don't sell any more or give any out either. It's important."

Chang and Moose don't say anything for a moment. I imagine them looking at each other, silently assessing my strange request.

"Look, Nix, it's a holiday weekend, Christmas in the MEEP," Moose finally says. "That's big business for us. Half the high school's texting us for overrides."

"Well don't give any more out," I insist, trying not to raise my voice. "Look, you guys, I'm not messing with you. It's dangerous. No more hacks."

"Where are you, Nixy?" Chang asks.

"Can't say."

"You're working for Diego Salvador, aren't you?"

"Why would you say that?" I snap, inwardly cursing the Spock-like Chang and bracing myself for the checkmate I know is coming.

"One, you don't have a great-aunt Martha. Two, my uncle is a janitor at the airstrip. He saw you and Vic board a Cessna Mustang this morning. And three, how else would you have inside information about the hack frequencies?"

"Whatever, Sherlock," I say. "Just do what I ask . . . *please*?"

"All right, we'll comply," Chang says, though I hear Moose groan in the background. "But you have to bow out, Nixy."

"What do you mean?"

"Don't do it, whatever Diego Salvador is asking you to do."

"Why not? It's good money, Chang, and I'm already here."

"So I was right," he says.

Damn. I just gave away my hand like an idiot.

"Think about it, Nixy," Chang continues. "If Salvador has hired *you* for a levelling job, that means no one else—not even his best programmers—could get the job done. Something's not right about that. You need to walk away."

"But it's his *son*," I say, figuring I might as well let the whole mewling cat out of the bag. Chang will figure it out sooner or later, just like he always does. "He's run away inside the MEEP and left a mess behind him."

"Then let Diego Salvador go in and find him. It's their mess, not yours. Let them deal with it. This is none of your business."

"Chang's right," says Moose, his voice serious now. "Let those rich people sort out their own problems. You need to come home, Nixy."

I sigh. "Look, guys, it's nothing I can't handle. And besides, Salvador employs both my parents. Just lay off the hacks until I get back, okay? I'll even split some of my paycheck with you. Gotta run."

"Nixy—" Chang starts, but I hang up before he can say anything else.

It's showtime.

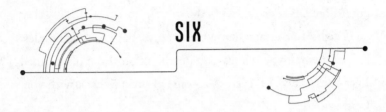

SIX

OKAY, SO WYN SALVADOR LOOKS LIKE A SLEEPING ANGEL, IF ANGELS are hot guys with long lashes and lips that beg to be kissed. This irritates me, as I'd rather he sported a jerk face when I give him the takedown he deserves.

An older woman sits at his side and smiles at me sadly. "He is a handsome boy, yes?"

I can't help but smile back at her. This must be Mama Beti, and she is, quite frankly, as adorable as her name. She wears a flowered cotton sundress and a matching yellow wrap around her head that shows off the fine angles of her face, the coffee-with-cream color of her skin, the deep brown eyes and long lashes. Both the Salvador men—father and son—obviously inherited their looks from this woman.

Mr. Salvador, Kora, and Dad are all huddled in the corner in front of a portable computer stand. Kora is tapping something into the keyboard while Dad and Salvador murmur behind her. Mama Beti sits in an overstuffed chair next to Wyn's bed, a sturdy metal walker parked nearby. She reaches an arm out to summon me. When I walk over to her she takes my hand in hers.

"You must find him for me," Mama Beti says in accented English. "He is not hiding, he is lost. Do you understand me, *linda*?"

I'm about to remind her my name is Nixy, not Linda, but then I remember from Spanish class that *linda* means "pretty," and I blush a little bit under her gaze. It is intense, this Mama Beti gaze.

"I'll find him, I promise," I tell her.

She squeezes my hand. "My grandson likes beautiful things. Maybe that will help you search for him. Look," she commands, sweeping a ropy yet elegant hand through the room.

I look around Wyn's room and I see what she means. Though the room is dominated by Wyn's bed and the IV machine attached to the needle in his arm, now I observe the ocean blue walls and white-painted bookshelves that display a large collection of baubles and seashells, polished rocks and exotic handicrafts, in addition to dozens of books on art and architecture. A huge picture window looks out at the sea. I have to admit, Wyn's room certainly isn't the typical teenage boy dump I usually encounter: clothes on the floor, empty soda cans, burrito wrappers, posters of sports teams or the TARDIS on the walls (depending), and an oversize computer monitor, extra-smudged.

"See? Beautiful things, like you," Mama Beti says. I run a hand through my hair and wonder if Mama Beti is sincere or just working me. I hold her gaze for a moment and decide she's sincere.

"Thank you," I say, then turn back to Wyn, who lies next to her. If it weren't for the IV hooked up to him, you'd think the guy was taking the sweetest nap in the world. The corners of his mouth are turned up a bit, as if he's dreaming of baby dolphins or a basket of kittens, rather than operating a virtual torture maze.

A servant comes in then, pushing what looks like a portable operating table. Kora directs him to the far end of the room near the bookshelves, but apparently Mama Beti has other plans.

"*Aquí*, Juanito," she calls, waving to the area on the other side of her chair. "This way, I look after you both," she says to me.

That's when I realize the operating table is for *me*. Dad sees my face and puts his hands on my shoulders. "There's still time to say no, Nixy. You don't have to do this."

I glance over at Mama Beti, who is kneading her hands in

worry. "I know, Dad, but I'm good at this, you know I am. I'll give it a try, but can we skip the ER drama?" I ask, pointing to the portable bed.

Kora chimes in. "It's just a precaution, Nixy, in case you're in the MEEP a little longer than expected. Your body will be more comfortable reclined on the hospital bed and we can monitor your vital signs more easily."

"My vital signs? Look, I'll be back within the hour. That's my thing. Two hours tops. Just tell me how to activate the return frequency once I find him," I say, looking back at Wyn.

Now Mr. Salvador speaks. "We've programmed an eleven-digit return frequency that you may use at any time. You can access the code from your inventory. Just read the numbers aloud into the MEEPosphere and it will immediately activate your return."

"Will the same code bring back Wyn?" I ask.

Mr. Salvador shakes his head. "No, unfortunately. Because he's tampered with his internal settings, we're unable to match frequencies with his ear trans. He'll have to initiate his own return."

"But what if he refuses to come back?" I ask.

Mr. Salvador raises his eyebrows at me. "I thought you were the expert in retrieval? Surely you can convince—or trick him."

Touché, big guy, I think, but then I look at Mama Beti and say, "I'll do my best."

"We've also given you unlimited credit in the Landing to equip yourself with any supplies and weaponry you feel you may need," Kora says.

"They've doubled your working inventory capacity as well," Dad says, "so you'll have a total of ten slots to carry what you need."

I whistle. Those are some decent perks. I hope I get to keep them once the job is done.

"Now if you'll please just lie down," says Kora, "we can get started."

I look at the hospital bed and shrug. Whatever. I feel my phone vibrate as I sit on the bed. Chang and Moose, certainly. They'll have to wait. I pull out the phone and power it down, then put it back in my pocket. I kick my shoes off and stretch out on the bed.

Kora gives me an ear trans.

Mama Beti reaches up and holds my hand.

Dad leans over to kiss me on the forehead. He looks like he's just put me on a train to Siberia to serve a life sentence.

I laugh. "It's just a game, Dad, no worries," I say, smiling up at him. "'Nixy Bauer, home in an hour,' remember?" I hear myself saying as the frequency starts beeping.

Christmas in the Landing is in full swing. The choir is belting out some jolly tune and a dance troupe of sugarplum fairies leaps around the Christmas tree. A forest elf tries to hand me a sales flyer and a sample potion for hot pink eyelash extensions. It's way too distracting and I don't need samples or discounts today. I've got unlimited credit, oh yeah! I walk straight to the Information Desk and look through my options on the main control panel. I press the WINTER SOLSTICE button, figuring that will be the least annoying backdrop to the mad dash I'm about to make through the mall.

There. Much better. No more tinsel and Christmas carols, just some boring new age music, snow-laden fir trees, and a few silver-clad druids drifting among the Meeple. I'm about to start shopping when another button on the panel lights up; apparently, Wyn has MEEP Mail. I hesitate for a moment, wondering if I should be reading his private messages, but then I decide he gave up all rights to common courtesy once he left his family behind. I quickly scan the mail, only to find it's for me.

NIXY, ABORT MISSION! TOO DANGEROUS!—CHANG

Unbelievable.

I know Chang's got some mad hacking skills, but this is crazy. Is there no code he can't unravel? I don't have time to ponder my friend's resourcefulness right now. I've got work to do.

I purse my lips and type a quick response:

NO.

That should do it.

I take a moment to review what's already in my working inventory. I've got the ultra crossbow, which I intend to keep, but I need to stock more arrows. I decide to keep my mage staff as well, but everything else I place in my storage locker to clear up space for new goods.

The MEEP MAIL button lights up again. "What part of NO do you not understand, Chang?" I grumble, pressing the button.

This time it's from Moose.

NIX, HERE'S THE DATA CHANG RECORDED FROM OUR MINI-GAMES.

I could hug Jackson Mooser right now. Attached to the message is a list of all the enemies we've fought in our mini-game sessions and the most effective weapons to defeat them. The perfect shopping list. I copy it to my inventory, laughing at Moose's last line:

SENDING YOU MY LUCKY POTATO GUN VIA POST.

I make a beeline to World of WarToys on the second floor, where I'll be making the majority of my purchases. I buy the best of everything, running through the list as fast as I can. Within minutes I've filled my storage locker with a decent variety of weapons and all the ammo I can pack.

Next I visit the I Will Survive! store and pick up a heavy-duty rappelling gun and harness, and the best pair of night-vision goggles I can find. My new contacts may not cut it for this gig.

I've now filled ninety-eight of the one hundred slots in my storage locker. I think about leaving them empty to save time, but the unlimited credit is burning a hole in my virtual pocket. I may never have this chance again. I hightail it to Medieval Moderne and buy the wench dress on my Wish List, then I figure, what the heck: I pop into the Parcel Post and pick up the potato gun delivery from Moose. I don't want to hurt his feelings, especially after he took the time to help me out.

I'm loaded for bear now. Or shark, as the case may be. I take a few minutes to browse my Closet and change into a casual commando outfit, basically a T-shirt, cargo pants, and boots, plus a leather holster belt. I arm myself with the things I'll need first, then fill the rest of my inventory slots with items from my locker.

It's time to go hunting.

No fear, no fear, no fear, I tell myself as I walk purposefully through the Landing to the portal. *It's just a game. They can't really eat you.*

The automatic portal doors sense my approach and slide open before me in friendly fashion, like they do at the grocery store. I pause for a second and mentally rehearse the next few moments. If I were in my physical body, I would take some deep breaths, try to slow my heart rate. But those things don't matter here. All that matters is how fast and how well my brain can instruct my virtual body to operate.

I step into the room and hear the doors whoosh shut behind me.

I glance around.

It's just like the MEEP-O Men said it would be: white everywhere, with no signs of entrance or exit. A few seconds later a message appears in black inky cursive across the walls:

Now begins the great adventure. Though I leave behind a body, my soul will live forever in the MEEP.

As the words begin to fade, I ready myself for what's coming next.

It happens faster than I expected.

The floor drops open and I fall.

I shoot my rappelling gun at the ceiling and brace myself for the jolt on the back of my harness. I hate to look down, but there's no time for cowardice.

Fy fæn.

Three fins circle in the water below me, less than three feet away. Two of the sharks are smaller or, perhaps more accurately, less ginormous than the third, who looks to be an 18-footer.

Suddenly I feel like a worm on the end of a hook. If he wanted to, Mr. 18 could easily breach the surface and pick me off faster than I can reach for my guns.

I start to panic, trying to make sense of the competing voices yelling at each other inside my brain.

GET THE HELL OUT OF HERE, NIXY!

NO! YOU CAN DO THIS!
INITIATE THE FREQUENCY CODE!
THEY'RE NOT REAL, DAMN IT!
SAY THE NUMBERS!
PULL OUT YOUR GUNS AND SHOOT!

I start blasting my two laser guns into the tank like I'm Yosemite Sam. The sharks whip into a frenzy, running into each other in the tank, thrashing around in a blur of gray. My initial panic begins to subside, replaced by the familiar head rush of battle. This isn't as hard as I thought it would be. A few more shots should do it.

And they do. The two smaller sharks eventually stop moving, and then they disappear. Now I've just got Mr. 18 to deal with.

Heh.

Only now he has more room in the tank. And he knows where I am.

The voices in my head have no time to argue. In a flash he breaches the surface. Two tons of gray flesh and a gaping maw of teeth come straight at me.

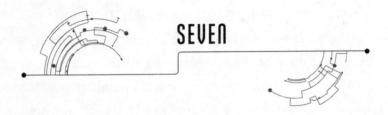

SEVEN

I SQUEEZE MY EYES SHUT AND BLAST BOTH LASER GUNS INTO HIS open jaws.

I hear a splash and take a quick peek through squinting eyes. I check to see if my legs are still attached to my body.

They are, thank God. I've been killed many times in virtual battle, but I've never been virtually eaten, and hope I never will be. Even though the logical part of my brain knows I won't feel any pain while it's happening and that I will regenerate within seconds, I don't think I can live with the image of my torso torn in half—my body being devoured limb by limb by an oversize guppy.

Below me the huge shark flails a few times, then stills and slowly dissolves in the water like an Alka-Seltzer.

I twirl around on my harness, waiting for what I've been told will happen next. Sure enough, the shark tank disappears and the white room returns.

"Inventory!" I command into the MEEPosphere, and my list of available items appears like a sidebar inside my head. I quickly trade my laser guns and rappelling equipment for a machete and a full supply of grenades.

A door slides open in front of me and I exit the room into the maze. The maze is all white too, corridors upon corridors, mostly leading to dead ends. But Dad and I went over my strategy step-by-step on the plane; I reach my right arm out and drag my fingers along the wall, always making right turns no matter what.

Within a few minutes, I discover a blue button on the wall. I mentally review my plan, then push the button. Another door appears and opens before me. As soon as I step inside, the door closes, and once again I'm trapped in a white box with no visible signs of entry or exit. When I reach the center of the room, the white turns into a hazy green and a second later I'm standing in the middle of a thick, overgrown jungle. I draw my machete and cautiously begin hacking my way through the claustrophobia-inducing foliage.

The jungle seems to throb with damp heat and buzzing insects. Close spaces aren't normally a problem for me, but still, it feels as though it's hard to breathe. Two thoughts take turns playing through my mind as I cut through ropy vines and giant fern-like plants. One, this is some impressive programming; I actually *feel* hot and sweaty and breathless. And two, I'm definitely not a save-the-rain-forest, Mother Nature kind of girl. I can't wait to get out of here, and fast.

As if on cue, I hear a slithering sound to my right and I whip my head around, machete at the ready. A streak of yellow shows through the green. Then *whooosh*, something flies by to my left, creating a breeze across my cheek. I whip my head left, but see nothing. *Slither, whoosh. Slither, whoosh.* My head is spinning like a top now as I turn from one side to the next, trying to follow the sounds.

These jungle creatures—two man-eating plants and a giant anaconda, according to the report—seem to be playing with me, *stalking* me. I feel my skin crawl, a sensation I've never felt in the MEEP before. For a fleeting second I wonder if they are monitoring my vital signs back in Wyn's room, and if so, whether my brow is beaded with sweat, my heart pounding triple-time.

I wonder, illogically, if any of this could take a physical toll. If it could, actually, *hurt* me somehow. *I need to end this* now, I think, *before I find myself swallowed whole and have a heart attack back in the real world.*

"It's just a game," I remind myself, as I take the machete in my left hand and ready a grenade with my right. I have to take out the plants first, according to the reports, as they're faster than the snake, and sneakier. The next time I hear a *whoosh*, I turn toward the sound and quickly lob the grenade in its general direction. I hear a muffled explosion and smell a burning odor. Yes! Contact! And even more amazing, I can smell something! In the MEEP!

But my delight is short-lived, as I immediately hear another *whoosh* from behind me. I whip around, fumbling for another grenade, but I'm stopped short by the horrifying sight of the second man-eating plant coming at me.

It almost looks like it could be Jack's beanstalk, if the stalk was a slimy, quivering tangle of pea-green intestines with a bulbous, kidney-colored, drooling *head* at the top.

Its open beak reveals a fleshy, pulsing void that reeks of rotting meat. I'm no longer thrilled by my ability to smell things here, and I sure as heck refuse to get swallowed whole by *that* stinkweed.

I whip out another grenade and lob it underhand, like I'm tossing a Ping-Pong ball into a fishbowl at the carnival. Bingo! Give the girl a prize. The carnivorous weed does a smoky little death dance, then begins to dissolve.

I'd like to wave good riddance, but who's got the time? I hear the slither before I can move the machete back to my right hand, so I end up making an awkward lefty slash behind me. I get nothing but air. A long, leathery tail wraps around my ankles and begins to encircle my legs, squeezing me from bottom to top like a tube of toothpaste. I figure it's only a matter of seconds before my rib cage gets crushed in the serpent's grip, sending me back to the Landing to start all over again.

That is *so* not going to happen.

I struggle to keep my arms free as long as possible and wait until I finally see the anaconda's big yellow head swaying in front of me, its tongue flicking in and out of its mouth, licking its lips before dinner, no doubt.

I take my machete in both hands and bring it down hard, like I'm cutting a watermelon in half.

The snake's head flies off into the jungle.

That's a nice line drive if I ever saw one.

"And the crowd goes wild," I say to no one, letting out a big sigh as the jungle finally disappears.

I pause a moment in the white room to put away the machete and remaining grenades, then I pull out my crossbow and quiver. I'm actually looking forward to this next room.

I follow the walls again, always turning right, until I reach a green button.

A moment later, I'm standing on a long rickety rope bridge between two high granite cliffs. Several planks are missing from the bridge, threatening to drop me into the sea of boiling orange lava below. I quickly don my harness and clip myself to the ropes before the first pterodactyl attacks.

The five dive-bombing dinos do their best to knock me into the lava gorge or spear me with their pointy beaks, but they are no match for this girl/weapon combo. My crossbow and I perform like a beautiful machine, a symphony of movement, a perfect, deadly blend of accuracy and precision. It's like the bow and I have morphed into one body—a Transformer, only cuter and less clunky.

We pick them off one by one, until the last one falls . . .

. . . onto the rope bridge.

Oops.

The bridge sags under the weight of the beaky bird, then snaps in two.

I'm already harnessed to one side of it, but I grab for the ropes anyway and we go swinging down like Tarzan, skim the boiling lava, and smash into the granite wall.

Ouch is all I have time to think before my skull cracks like an egg.

I wake up in the Landing. "Wyn Salvador, you son of a *rasshøl*!" I yell into the mall. I know it isn't very nice, but I don't care. At this point I thoroughly despise Wyn Salvador and his creepy fright fest. And now I have to start over again. I just lost thirty valuable minutes of time, not to mention a piece of my sanity. No wonder some of the MEEP-Os ended up mental.

I fly through the Landing, reloading on ammunition and supplies. It's one thing to create your own game in the MEEP, to *know* who your enemies will be before you go in. Like those Choose Your Own Adventure books for kids. Let's say you decide to battle a dragon. You still feel a thrill of fear once that dragon starts chasing you with his razor-sharp claws and fiery breath, but at least you *chose* him, and if you're any good, you also equipped yourself with some decent weaponry to fight him. It's another thing entirely to battle unknown enemies that another player chose. It's like someone telling you there's a monster under your bed, then forcing you to stick your head down there to look.

There aren't enough chill pills in the world to get over that kind of mind game.

But I'm not giving up yet. Not now that I know how to play.

I race through the stores—more grenades, more arrows, extra batteries for the laser guns, and after much rumination, I trade in the mage staff for a Santa Claus fat suit from the Custom Costume shop.

I have my reasons.

I'm on a mission now to haul Wyn Salvador's sorry butt back home so I can swear at him in person and make him grovel for mercy.

I go back to the portal, arm myself, and start over.

●—●—●

This time around I kill off the sharks, plants, and snake with speed and efficiency. I'm nowhere near as anxious on this run because I know what to expect. It's still pretty terrifying, of course, but I just keep repeating my mantra whenever the fear starts to take over: *It's just a game, it's just a game, it's just a game.* . . .

I take down the pterodactyls even faster this time, and when the last one slams onto the bridge, I'm ready for it. I equip the Santa suit with lightning speed and let out a victorious "HO HO HO!" as I careen toward the granite cliff, waiting for my fat suit to cushion the impact.

I bounce a few times off the wall like a big red Super Ball, and I let out a laugh, wishing Chang and Moose were here to see this amazing Christmas miracle.

I stop laughing when I hear a *SNAP* above me. I'm so heavy in the fat suit that I've ripped the bridge off its moorings at the top of the cliff.

Down we go, bridge and all, straight into the boiling lava.

I don't yell this time when I wake up in the Landing. Instead, I allow myself to daydream about all the things I will say to Wyn Salvador when I find him. They are very unpleasant things, things that should never ever be uttered aloud, lest you be struck dead by whichever God is currently on duty. It's a risk I'm willing to take.

Once again I run through the Landing and restock, occasionally muttering at the strolling Meeple in their natural-fiber Winter Solstice wear. They just smile at me and continue strolling, presumably filled with the spirit of the Winter Goddess or Nature or something Peaceful and Seasony. In contrast, I am filled with rage, which I try to channel into cold, hard determination. I open my storage locker to trade the damn Santa suit for my mage staff, but in my haste I access the potato gun instead. *What the hell?* I think, leaving it in my inventory. Maybe it'll bring me luck, like Moose says, and God knows I'm ready for some.

This time, I kill the sharks before they know I'm there. The man-eating plants are toast after the first *whoosh*; the anaconda doesn't even have time to slither. I make sure to shoot the five wheeling pterodactyls at the three-o'clock or nine-o'clock positions, so they fall straight into the lava and stay away from my bridge.

Finally, the lava gorge dissolves to white.

Victory at last. I stand still for a few minutes, allowing plenty of time to prep myself for the next room. I've already blown my "Nixy Bauer, Home in an Hour" 5K bonus, so the extra time doesn't make a difference anymore. Besides, this is the *fourth* room, the room where the MEEP-O Men before me died a thousand deaths before giving up in defeat. I'm determined to win this one the first time through, as a point of pride.

Also, I'll scream if I wake up in the Landing one more time.

I equip myself with an oak shield and a razor-sharp Gladius sword. Just before I push the yellow button to the next room, I swallow down the pricey speed potion I acquired just for this purpose.

The whiteness turns into a golden haze, and it takes me a moment to get my bearings. I'm in a desert, melting hot, and the sun shines brightly into my eyes. I spin around in a circle to mark the location of my foes. "Just like the three bears," Dad had said on the plane, "and you're Goldilocks," he added, while we were strategizing my attack. I laughed at the time and said I hoped they served a decent porridge, but it doesn't seem nearly as funny now. Bears would be a welcome sight.

Giant scorpions? Not so much.

I see them now, right where they're supposed to be. Papa is at four o'clock, shiny and black and the biggest of them, his stinger raised to a height about twice my own five feet ten inches. Mama's at eight o'clock, copper-tinted and moving slowly, biding her sweet time. And Baby's positioned directly at twelve o'clock, an iridescent greenish blue like a dragonfly and the smallest of the three, but also the fastest and coming right at me.

"Okay, let's get this done," I say to myself. I run as fast as I can toward Baby, my sword high in the air. I move like a panther, my legs pumping at least twice their normal speed, and I feel like I'm about to go airborne. I've never used a speed potion before—performance enhancements have always been *way* out of my price range—and it almost feels like cheating.

Baby sees me and raises his stinger even higher without losing speed. I can't believe I'm playing a game of chicken with a giant scorpion, but here we are, running at each other like freight trains about to collide. "Wait for it . . . wait for it," I mutter to myself as we get closer and closer, and then *SWISH*, down comes his stinger, straight at my heart.

I whip up the oak shield just in time, and sink to my knees as the stinger plunges into the wood. It makes a loud *THUNK*, then Baby lets out an even louder high-pitched screech when he realizes he's stuck. For a second I wonder if scorpions screech in real life, but then Baby lifts his tail with both me and my shield still attached, and my mind snaps back to the task at hand. I bring down the Gladius sword as hard as I can and slice Baby's tail clean off.

Baby lets out one last screech before he dissolves into thin air and I fall to the sand. There's no time to brush myself off. If Papa and Mama were dangerous before, they're in a murderous rage now. They come charging at me from opposite sides and it's all I can do to hold my ground between them.

They skitter around me, their black-and-copper stingers raining down in syncopated rhythm. Two Papa strikes for every Mama strike. As I tumble and dodge, flipping in between their tails like a Chinese acrobat on speed, I take note of their movements. Papa's strikes are more forceful and rapid, but Mama's got accuracy going for her.

Just as Papa raises his tail to strike again, I roll myself between Mama's coppery legs. *CRUNCH*. Papa's stinger plunges itself into Mama's back. Mama screeches and her body goes into defensive auto-pilot. I hear another *CRUNCH* as her stinger plunges into Papa.

Papa doesn't even complain, he just takes it like a boss and dissolves into the sand, locked in the fatal embrace of his wife.

Whew.

I sit down, shading myself with the oak shield until the desert turns back into the white room. I am exultant for a minute before a hideous realization descends on me like a school of poison jellyfish. If I weren't virtual, I would shiver. The known portions of the maze are now complete. From here on out, I don't know what to expect, how to equip myself, or what kind of monsters to watch for. It's all guesswork. And if I fail, it's back to the beginning. All of it—all over again.

It's enough to make a weaker person, a person who in no way resembles *me*, cry.

I tap into my inventory and take a look around. I change my mind several times, then finally decide to arm myself with the rappelling gun and crossbow. Fight and flight, both covered. I can always trade weapons mid-challenge, though that's often the best way to lose. In battle, every second is precious.

I follow the white wall, which has become like my own yellow brick road, without a comforting trio of friends or trusty dog to help me out. I snort for a quick second, imagining Hodee trying to keep up with Dorothy on his squat legs as she skipped and danced around in those red ruby slippers. Nope, Hodee wouldn't have made it past Munchkinland. On the flip side, there's not a flying monkey alive who could have lifted his roly-poly body off the ground. Toto 1, Hodee 1.

These images amuse me through several twists and turns of the maze until I finally reach a red button. I close my eyes and try to focus, ridding myself of Oz and dogs and other thoughts that might distract me from whatever comes next.

I push the button and step into the room, crossbow cocked and ready.

A face begins to appear on the white wall in front of me. It's a pretty woman's face, pleasant and smiling and all-American, like the kind you see in TV commercials for Oil of Olay.

"Checkpoint complete," she says in a soothing, robotic voice. "Checkpoint complete."

Praise the Lord and pass the life hearts! Wyn Salvador actually included save points in this horrid little game. I will not have to face those stinking sharks again, let alone all the other creatures. I'm so happy I could cry. I smile back at the nice checkpoint lady. Maybe she'll take me to Wyn.

Only now her face doesn't look as pleasant as it did a second ago. Her eyes are turning red and her hair is turning white. Her teeth begin to . . . sharpen? . . . transforming her pleasant smile into a creepy, evil grin, as if she is now selling one-way bus tickets on the highway to hell.

I instinctively raise my crossbow, though she is no more than a projection.

The lights go out. I drown in the pitch darkness.

Panic freezes me to the spot until something in my brain kicks into gear.

"Inventory," I yell, and quickly access the night-vision goggles Dad had insisted I carry. "He's feeding on phobias, Nixy, and fear of the dark is a huge one," Dad had said on the plane just a few hours earlier, though it now feels like forever ago. "Remember how you used to turn on not one but three night-lights in your bedroom?"

I didn't say so to him, but sometimes I *still* sleep with three night-lights. After today I'm going to need four.

"It's just a game, it's just a game," I repeat to myself as I slip the goggles over my head. Half of me can't wait to put them on so I can see what the hell I'm up against. The other half doesn't want to know.

"*Fy fæn!*" I yell, and jump right out of my skin.

The hag is directly in front of me, her demonic face inches from mine. An icy coldness seeps from her body like a thick fog. I feel like I've just stepped into a deep freeze.

"RUN!" she screams, her hideous voice stabbing my ears like a dagger.

She doesn't need to tell me twice. I take off.

The door to the room is open and I run back into the maze, which is now steeped in darkness. The night-vision goggles turn everything a ghoulish green. I run wildly, terrified of what I might find ahead of me, but even more horrified by what's behind me. I risk a quick peek back and wish I hadn't. The woman is flying behind me like a ghostly white witch, her teeth bared in that horrible grin. Her long bony arms stretch out before her, and her hands, which look more like sharp talons, try to grab me. She starts to cackle then, louder and louder until the cackle turns into a high-pitched shriek that makes my head feel like it might explode.

I run left and right and this way and that, completely lost, completely out of my wits. I can't think straight, can't do anything but try to outrun her outstretched claws, her hideous shrieking. I make another left and hit a dead end.

I feel her icy hands scrape across my back. Her talons cut through cloth and bone and a searing cold permeates my chest, freezing and burning all at once.

She's ripping my heart out, my mind screams as I slip into unconsciousness.

Yep. Dead end.

Literally.

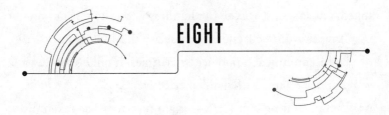

EIGHT

WHEN I WAKE UP, I'M BACK IN THE WHITE ROOM WITH OIL OF OLAY LADY smiling at me from the wall. Damn. No rest for the wicked. I reposition my goggles, load my crossbow, and wait for the lights to go out.

A second later, all is dark. Leering banshee straight ahead.

I aim an arrow at her horrible mouth. *THWACK!*

It goes right through her.

"RUN!" she screams.

Oh God.

I run. I can't help it. I can't bear the thought of those icy hands reaching into my body again. I shouldn't be able to feel them. Why *can* I feel them? I'm not sure I even care at this point. I try to keep my hand along the right wall, always going right, but the inky green darkness confuses me, the night-vision goggles mess with my peripheral vision.

Think, think, think, Nixy.

I try to remember what's left in my inventory as I run. Not much. I need to get back to the Landing and restock, but how?

"Inventory!" I yell, and arm myself with a laser gun.

I whirl around and pop her three times. It's like shooting a water gun at a piranha. Totally ineffective.

I keep running, but I'm lost again now that I've taken my hand off the right wall to shoot.

Damn damn damn.

I toss a grenade behind me. The banshee only shrieks louder.

I don't even notice the dead end this time until I run smack into it.

I feel a frosty stab of pain enter between my shoulder blades, like I've just been impaled by an icicle.

She steals my heart again.

I do the same thing twelve times in all, with slight variations. Each time, I try another weapon from my inventory on the witch. Gladius sword, rappelling gun, machete, more grenades. I might as well be battling whipped cream or clouds, only not so fluffy and pleasing.

Twelve times the lights go out; twelve times her ghoulish

face appears inches from my own; twelve times I try to kill her with something; twelve times she doesn't die; twelve times she screams "RUN!"; twelve times I run like my pants are on fire; twelve times I get lost; twelve times I feel her arctic claw reach inside my rib cage and rip my heart out.

Twelve flipping times I want to give up and yell out my return code frequency. But I'm not a quitter. I remember when I was little, maybe eight years old, and I was playing a Zelda game on Dad's old Nintendo. It took me twenty-eight attempts to beat Ganon, the final boss at the end. I remember begging my dad to fight the battle for me, but all he said was, "Keep at it, Nixinator. Each time you try, you sweeten the victory." And it was true. That twenty-ninth attempt—that *successful* attempt—was so incredibly delicious that I jumped on my bed for ten minutes afterward out of pure happiness.

As I prepare for my lucky—ha ha—thirteenth try, I tap into my inventory once again and try desperately to think of some trick, some new thing, something "out of the box" to defeat the Hag of Olay, but once again I don't have *time* to think. The lights go out and the ghoulfriend's in my face again screaming "RUN!"

I haven't even armed myself this time. I access my inventory and grab the first weapon I can get to. I look down to find the potato gun in my hands. Oh for God's sake.

It's so absurd I start laughing. I look right into the banshee's red eyes and only flinch slightly. I've looked into her hideous face so many times now I'm getting used to it. Might as well skip to the chase at this point, or skip the chase altogether, as the case happens to be. "Go ahead," I say, sticking out my chest. "Just rip it right out."

We both stand there for a moment—technically, I guess, the banshee floats—and engage in an intense staring contest. I am really good at this game, honed by hours of matches with Moose during eighth-grade study hall. I blow a puff of air into her eyes, and her icy eyelids flutter. "Made you blink," I sing, mainly to amuse myself while I wait for the heart snatchery that is to come.

Only it doesn't.

The banshee backs away from me and the lights go back on. I remove my night-vision goggles and see the white wall swallow her up until only her face is showing . . . her horrible, witchy face, which slowly transforms back into my favorite smiling, well-moisturized lady.

"Checkpoint complete," says the soothing robotic voice. "Checkpoint complete."

I'm almost too stunned to move.

I don't know what happened back there, but I'm pretty sure I can now add Blinking Contest Goddess to my college applications.

A door in the white wall slides open and I see what looks

like a room full of Meeple on the other side.

"You've got to be kidding me," I mutter, stepping tentatively across the threshold and looking around in wonder.

Yep. I'm in a bar.

Not just any bar either, but a really swank one populated by happy, beautiful Meeple, sitting at a long, glossy counter and raising shiny glasses at each other. They all look fabulous in a sort of half-retro, half-exotic way, like we're at some kind of tropical sock hop. Some of the Meeple are speaking English and others are speaking Spanish, I think, unless it's Italian. Or Portuguese. Obviously I need to pay more attention to Señora Jorgen in Español III.

"Welcome to the Floridita. What can I get for you, señorita?" asks a nice-looking, red-coated bartender.

I open my mouth to respond, but nothing comes out. My brain can't seem to wrap itself around the fact that A) I'm out of immediate danger, and B) I'm in a *bar*, for Pete's sake, and apparently, no one's going to card me.

"Mix the girl a daiquiri, Chucho, and put it on my bill," says a big, white-haired, white-bearded guy from the end of the bar. He gives me a flirtatious wink, then turns back to the man sitting next to him. I know it's rude to stare, even if they are Meeple, but I can't help it. Both men look so familiar.

"Is that—?" I say, hoisting myself onto a bar stool.

Chucho starts pouring rum, lime juice, ice, and something

else into a shaker. "Señor Hemingway, *sí*. Ernesto's a regular here and he often brings his American guests, like Señor Tracy there."

I nod, remembering now. We had to read some of Ernest Hemingway's short stories last year in English class. They were my favorites. Nice and lean, not a lot of extra words. After the dark hell that was Nathaniel Hawthorne's *Scarlet Letter*, Hemingway's stories seemed pleasingly crisp and clean.

"He can buy me a drink and wink at me anytime. He's earned it," I say to Chucho, whose Meeple script doesn't know how to respond to this last utterance of mine.

Chucho just smiles at me and shakes my drink in a metal canister. I like the sound it makes.

"And Señor Tracy?" I ask, not recognizing the name. "Who is he?"

"That is Spencer Tracy, señorita, the big movie star from America!"

"Oh, right," I say, taking another glance down at the end of the bar. No wonder I had a hard time placing him. I've only seen Spencer Tracy in black-and-white movies, when it's Chang's turn to choose the lineup for our weekly Friday-night TV binge.

Chucho slides me a martini glass filled with an icy lime-green concoction. Even though you can't taste things in the MEEP, it feels impolite not to take a sip.

I do, and nearly choke. "I can taste this!" I exclaim, making the men chuckle at the end of the bar.

"Chucho makes very good daiquiri, no?" says Chucho himself, his eyebrows raised in question.

"It's *delicioso*," I assure him, then take another sip of the cold liquid, sweet and tart at the same time. How is this possible?

"Chucho, where are we? Is this Miami?" I ask, looking around at the smartly dressed Meeple, especially the women with their beehive hairdos and penciled eyebrows. "And *when* are we, for that matter?"

"Señorita, we are in the one and only Havana, Cuba. The year is 1958. Another drink?"

"No, no thank you," I say, finishing off the last few drops of my daiquiri and hopping off the stool. Thankfully, I don't feel tipsy at all from the virtual alcohol; I've wasted enough time. I need to figure out what the hell is going on, and fast. If this is the custom world that Wyn has created, he'll be here somewhere. I spin a quick 360 to take a good look at the rest of the bar. There are two doors in the back, including the one I came through, and another big door in front.

"So that's *Havana* out there?" I ask, pointing my chin toward the front door.

"*Sí*, señorita."

I smile at Chucho. He is starting to look familiar too,

somehow. "Anything I need to worry about out there? Anything . . . dangerous?" I ask, trying to remember the date of the Cuban Revolution. Maybe Wyn's fantasy is to be some Che Guevara revolutionary type.

"No, no, a few tough guys here and there, but they shouldn't bother you," Chucho says. "You go to the Tropicana, watch a show, maybe dance a little. Tell the doorman Chucho sent you and he'll take care of you, no worries."

I look at Chucho's smooth coffee-with-cream complexion, his warm brown eyes, his long lashes. Maybe I've seen him in an old movie too? I look a little longer and then it hits me. He's the spitting image of Mama Beti. Younger, and male, of course, but the similarities are definitely there. This *has* to be Wyn's custom world.

"You don't happen to know a guy named Wyn Salvador, do you?" I ask the smiling bartender.

"*Claro que sí*, señorita, Wyn is a regular around here. Nice fellow."

Bingo. "Do you know where he is now?"

Chucho looks at his watch. "No, but come back again tomorrow. I tell him to wait for you here, Señorita—?" he asks, waiting for my name.

"No need, Chucho! *Gracias!*" I say, showing off one of the few Spanish vocab words I can remember at the moment. "*Adios!*" I add, to further impress him with my fluency.

I wave to Ernesto and Spencer and head through the front

door. I'm shocked to realize it's nighttime, and I wonder if this MEEP's time zone has been synced to real world time. If so, I've been gone longer than I thought.

I'm at the corner of an intersection, where streetlights and headlights and neon signs light up the tall, balconied buildings lining the streets. The cars are big and wide and old-timey, with giant chrome fenders and hood ornaments, and painted with pretty pastel colors. Meeple stroll the streets, smiling and laughing, like they're all off to a party and not just strings of code. The air is warm, but a cool breeze blows, smelling of the sea. Again, I am astounded. I can *smell* things in this MEEP, feel and taste things. I'm also confused. I have no idea where to go, or how this world has been mapped. Also, given the dozens of Meeple walking around, Wyn could easily hide himself among them.

I start following a group of young Meeple up the street. The young men are dressed in lightweight suits and ties, while the girls wear smoking-hot dresses that cling to their curves. Maybe they'll lead me to Wyn. If there's one thing I've learned about levelling teenage boys, it's this: when in doubt, follow the hot girls.

We turn down a few more streets and now I can hear music throbbing from several clubs—bongo drums, maracas, and pianos all at once. I wonder if one of these clubs might be the Tropicana place that Chucho mentioned.

"Don't turn around," says a gruff voice from behind me as I feel cold metal on the back of my neck. "Keep walking and keep quiet."

"Oh please," I mutter under my breath. I was almost enjoying this custom MEEP world, but now I'm being mugged by some virtual Cuban thug. Oh well, it's better than a shark tank, and maybe this will lead me to Wyn. He's probably made himself a mob boss or something.

"Where are we going?" I ask, as he pushes me down a narrow alley. "And do they serve daiquiris there?" I joke, more for my own amusement than his. Most Meeple have a limited capacity to understand sarcasm.

"In there," the voice says, directing me toward a door at the end of the alley. I open the door and the thug pushes me through a dark hallway and into another room. It appears to be a dressing room, and by the looks of the clothing strewn about, the woman who dresses here wears a lot of sequins, feathers, and . . . not much else.

"This must be your mother's room," I remark, wondering how the MEEP thug will reply.

"My mother's dead, but she preferred cottons while she was alive."

I twirl around then, not caring about the gun on my neck. Meeple don't talk like that. I recognize him immediately and fury overwhelms me.

"Wyn Salvador, you little pantywaist," I say, and charge him, despite the gun aimed directly at my head.

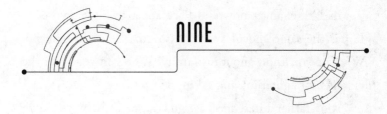

NINE

SURPRISE IS ON MY SIDE, FORTUNATELY, BECAUSE WYN SALVADOR isn't quite the pantywaist I just called him. I'm tall, but he's still got several inches of height on me, and seems pretty athletic.

I've got speed, though, and I know where to land a kick.

I kick *hard*.

The blow makes him drop the gun, which I snatch up and aim at his head this time.

"Your twisted game is over now," I say, as he slumps back against the wall and contemplates me. "I suggest you activate your return frequency this minute before I shoot you back home."

"Who are you?" he asks in a demanding tone, his face unreadable.

"Doesn't matter," I say, waving the gun at him. "You're wanted home immediately. Your family's been worried sick about you while you run around in your playground like a little brat."

His face changes now and I see anger in his brown eyes. He has the same chocolaty eyes as Mama Beti and Chucho. "What do you know about my family? Who sent you here?" he demands, straightening and taking a step forward.

"Your father hired me." I sigh, exasperated by the time we're wasting. "And I'm ready to collect my paycheck, so let's move it, bad boy."

Wyn stares at me in disbelief. "My father hired *you*? A teenage girl?" he asks.

It takes all of my self-control not to give Wyn Salvador another swift kick. I keep steady, but can't stop my mouth from tearing into him. "Yes, he *did*, in fact, hire *me*, a *girl*. Nobody else could get through your creepy maze, you freak show, and believe me, you're making me sorry I ever tried. Next time you run away, maybe you should think about all the people you're hurting first. Like Mama Beti. She's been sitting by your bedside night and day, you know, *missing* you, not to mention your dad and all the guilt he feels from your suicide note, or whatever it was."

As I yell, Wyn's face turns from anger to confusion. "They think I ran away?"

"Well, didn't you?"

Wyn doesn't answer my question. Instead he walks toward me, ignoring the gun, and grabs my shoulders. "Take me back right now. Show me how to go home." His face is scary intense and he's making me nervous.

"Wait—what for?" Now I'm confused.

He lets out a frustrated grunt. "Show me how you got in."

"I told you, I went through your damn maze."

"I don't know what you're talking about. A maze? Where? How does it work? Can we go back through it?" he asks, his hands still gripping my shoulders, his face inches from mine.

The maze . . .

I remember that flame-eyed witch ripping through my skin—the burn of her icy-cold fingers. If I have to feel that one more time, I . . .

I pull away from him. "No way. I am not going through that again. Look, just reverse whatever frequency you used to get here in the first place."

"Don't you think I've tried that?" he asks, his dark eyes flashing at me. "I'm trapped here. I've been trying to escape for days. Somebody's keeping me imprisoned here and I don't know why. Now show me the maze. Please. I've tried everything else I can think of."

I open my mouth, then close it again. So Wyn *wants* to go home?

The story of the wayward billionaire's son just got a little more interesting, but I decide to wait and ask for details once we get home. Right now we're on a tight schedule.

"What if I just shoot you?" I ask, waving the gun at him. "Maybe that will reset you back at the Landing."

Wyn shakes his head impatiently and taps his temple with his forefinger like it's the barrel of a gun. "Tried it. Doesn't work. I just blank out for a minute, then wake up in exactly the same place I started. With a wicked headache."

Whoa. I have never heard of anyone committing suicide in the MEEP before. And if the ordeal of the white witch was any indication, Wyn's actions caused him a not-inconsiderable amount of pain.

What he is saying begins to seep through my thick skull and into my cortex.

"You're really . . . you're *trapped* here?"

"That's what I've been trying to tell you, yes!"

My mind begins to race. Everything is different now.

"There must be another way out, something you haven't thought of," I say, dropping the useless gun and looking through my inventory. "Let me think."

"I'm telling you, *there's no other way*." He stares at me and begins to speak very slowly, as if I'm a small child. "Someone has trapped me here. I have been trying to escape for days. Show. Me. The. Maze."

I blow out my breath. "Fine, I'll show it to you, but we'll never make it through. I blew nearly all my ammo getting here, and I don't suppose you've got an unlimited supply either if you've been shooting yourself in the head."

Wyn glares at me. "I don't usually bring weapons to the MEEP. The gun's all I have, plus a few rounds of ammo."

I almost laugh. "Yeah, well I'm afraid that sharks and giant scorpions require a little more than a Colt .45."

Wyn tilts his head in disbelief. "Sharks. And scorpions?"

"Oh, that's not the half of it. So cool your jets for a minute and let me think, okay?"

Wyn paces for a few seconds in frustration, then leans against the wall and slides down to a sitting position. He rubs a hand over his face. "So how were you planning to return yourself, if not by the maze?"

"Your father gave me an emergency code. It won't work for you because you've tampered with your ear trans."

Wyn lifts his head. "I'm not the one who tampered with it."

"Either way," I say. "It won't work. It's not coded to your trans."

"Why don't they just shut down the game for a few minutes?" asks Wyn. "If everyone is as worried about me as you say, why doesn't my father just turn off the MEEP?"

I snort. "I see your father has kept his dirty little secret from you."

"What are you talking about?"

"Apparently there's a pesky side effect." I push some bright, feathery boas off a wooden table and hike myself onto the surface, sitting cross-legged. "Anybody playing the MEEP using nonregulation frequencies could suffer brain damage if the game is shut down."

Wyn grimaces, though he does not look very surprised. "I wondered about that," he says. "The brain's incredibly complex. . . . My father's people have done a lot of research but our neural paths are like an infinite universe."

"Yeah, well, easy to say now, Einstein. Maybe your father and his *people* should have let players know about the dangers involved instead of treating us like guinea pigs." I think of Chang and Moose, and wish they were here right now to help me figure this out.

"You don't know what you're talking about. My father's brain stem research has the potential to change the world," Wyn says. "True innovation always involves a certain amount of risk."

I get mad all over again. "Look, hotshot, you have no idea what I just went through. I've always loved the MEEP, as a *game* . . . but in one single day I've made two important discoveries. First, your father's 'innovation' has the potential to put people—people like *us*—in a coma. And second, it can be used to torture people. That maze would send most people into lifelong therapy."

Wyn doesn't look convinced. "People get 'killed' in games all the time. That's one of the reasons they play, isn't it? For the thrill, the adrenaline rush. How is that maze any different?"

"Because I didn't get to *choose* any of it. Half the time I didn't know what was coming. Don't you understand? It's like your worst nightmare, only a billion times worse because it feels so real."

"Still, it can't be that scary if you know it's a game," Wyn says with a shrug. I want to punch him.

"Fine, let's go, then," I say, hopping off the table.

Wyn gets to his feet. "Where to?"

"You want to go to the maze, I'll take you there. Be my guest," I say. Before meeting Wyn I wouldn't have wished the maze on my worst enemy, but now I can't wait for him to give it a go. Wyn Salvador is just as arrogant as his father. Let him be the shark bait and see how he feels.

He follows me to the alley, a small grin on his face like he's just won the battle. He has no idea. I look around to get my bearings once we reach the intersection. The street is still busy with festive Meeple and glowing neon signs advertising beer and cigarettes.

"We need to get to the Floridita bar and your pal Chucho," I say.

Wyn raises his eyebrows, then points left. "This way," he says, and we begin to make our way down the busy street.

As I follow Wyn, I take a good look around at the world he created. I have to admit, it's the best custom MEEP I've ever been in, certainly much more extravagant and vast than anything I've ever made. The buildings we pass have all been meticulously detailed, with their shadowy colonnades, their weathered paint, the scrolled ironwork of outdoor hanging lamps, gates, and balconies. I glance through one of the ground-floor gates and see a garden courtyard tucked between two buildings, where a Meeple couple sits and holds hands among the white flower bushes. A breeze floats across my cheeks and I smell a salty-sweet combination of ocean and flowers.

"That's amazing," I say, stopping to breathe in the delicious scent.

"Gardenias and Sea Breeze," Wyn says, his tone a little friendlier now. "The aroma modules are my favorite things to experiment with lately. I installed a bakery last week just so I could try out Buttery Croissants and Cinnamon Apple Pie."

"Can you taste them as well?" I ask, thinking of the delicious daiquiri.

Wyn nods. "It's not as good as eating the real thing. . . . The programmers are still playing around with texture, but it's a start."

My previous anger has dissipated somewhat during our stroll, and now I'm almost tempted to ask if we can hit the bakery before we go back home. But I remember my mission and pull myself together. My job is to get this guy home, not stop for pie.

"Look," I begin, "I don't know how the maze works in reverse, whether you'll start with the banshee or the sharks, but regardless, you're going to need a rappelling gun. You can borrow mine, assuming you don't have one."

I continue talking, telling him about each room of the maze and how to defeat the enemies within. The odds of him making it all the way through are a long shot, and I'm guessing he'll give up sooner rather than later once he sees what he's up against. But if he's that determined to try, I might as well let him give it a go. In the meantime, I can stay behind and try to think of another way out. "For the pterodactyls, you're going to need a—"

Wyn takes me by the arm and stops me in my tracks. We've reached a busy intersection and as we wait for the lights to change, he turns and smiles at me. I'm still mad at him, but it's the first time I've seen him smile—really smile—and I can't help it. My stomach does a little flip-flop. Wyn Salvador is . . . well, he's not hard on the eyes. Damn it.

"I still don't know your name," he says softly.

"Nixy," I say. "Nixy Bauer."

"Thank you, Nixy, for coming to my rescue." His brown eyes seem to sparkle at me and I feel my cheeks start to warm. I quickly look away from him, even though I know the blush I feel inside won't show on my avatar. At least I don't think it will.

The light changes and we walk across the intersection, his hand still wrapped around my arm. "I'll wait for you at the bar with Chucho," I say, trying to compose myself and steer the conversation back to practical matters. "I'm guessing that's where the maze will spit you out each time you die."

Wyn shivers a bit at this, but when I look over at him, he grins. "Nixy Bauer. Oh ye of little faith."

"Hey, nobody will be more pleased than me if you make it through in one try. The faster you get home, the faster I collect my paycheck."

"How will you know I've made it back?" he asks.

I've already thought of that. "Tell your dad to activate my emergency code remotely. That should work."

"And if it doesn't?"

I shrug. "Then I'll activate it myself after a few daiquiris with Chucho."

Wyn laughs. "Sounds like a plan."

We reach the Floridita and Wyn opens the door for me. I am beginning to enjoy his gentlemanly manners. Ernesto is still at the end of the bar, but is now completely engrossed by a gorgeous blonde. Wyn sees me looking and grins.

"Who's the dame with Hemingway?" I ask, waving to Chucho. "And why does the bartender look like your grand-mother?"

"When we get back to the real world, I'll buy you a milk shake and tell you all about it," he says.

"We'll see about that," I say. I try to keep my face neutral, but a smile pops through anyway.

We take a minute to trade inventory items, then I lead him to the back of the bar.

"This is it," I say, as we reach the door marked DAMAS. "Are you ready?"

Wyn glances at the sign and pretends to gasp. "The ladies' room? You're right, this *is* scary."

"You have no idea," I say, actually feeling sorry for what he's about to experience. "Good lu—" I begin, but before I can finish, he gives me a roguish wink and barrels through the bathroom door.

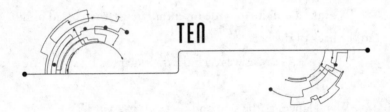

TEN

I CAN'T HELP IT. NOT EVEN TEN SECONDS HAVE PASSED AND I PEEK through the door.

I'm expecting a room of white. Instead I see a ladies' restroom with Wyn standing in the middle of it, legs apart, rappelling gun in one hand, laser gun in the other. He sees me in the doorway.

"How long does it take?" he asks, his eyes scanning the bathroom. "Do I have to press a button or something? Flush a toilet?"

"No," I say. "No, no, no, no, no." I look around in disbelief. I don't know whether to be horrified or relieved. "It's gone."

"What?" Wyn quits his "ready" stance and heads for the door. "Maybe you got it mixed up."

"I don't think so," I say testily, following him out. He opens the neighboring door that says HOMBRES and sticks his head in. "No sharks in there either?" I ask when he turns back around.

"Not unless they're in the sink." He blows out a long breath and runs a hand through his hair. "No sharks. Now what?"

"There must be another way to get you back. Try your return frequency code again."

"You know it doesn't work."

"Try it anyway."

He rolls his eyes, but dutifully recites the eleven-digit code loudly into the MEEPosphere. Nothing happens. "Satisfied?" he asks, crossing his arms over his chest.

"Wait a minute. How do you normally get to the Landing? Not through the restroom, I presume."

Wyn shakes his head at me and lets out a frustrated sigh. "You're not listening, are you? They've blocked all exits, Nixy. There's no way out."

"There must be," I say. "Take me to your Landing portal."

"Fine," Wyn says. "Come on."

We go back into the streets of Havana and walk for about five minutes before we turn down what looks like an older residential avenue. The two- and three-story buildings are all pressed together along the street, their balconies draped with flowers, the streetlights showing off their rainbow of colors. They look like a parade of frosted cakes with buttercream icing.

It's pretty here, even in the dark.

"Where are we?" I ask, as Wyn leads me inside one of the homes.

He doesn't answer. I continue to follow him through the front room of the dark house and up a wide staircase with a sleek wooden handrail. As we go up, he lights the electric sconces hung along the staircase wall, and I now see that the inside of the house is as pretty as the outside. The walls of the stairwell are painted a sea green and hung with dozens of framed portraits and landscapes. In the front room below I see small potted trees and urns of cut flowers sprinkled among the furniture, filling the house with color and more sweet smells. Wyn has been busy with the aroma modules here, too, I see.

We walk up two flights of steps until we get to the third floor, then enter the darkened room at the front of the house, the one facing the street. The balconied floor-to-ceiling windows stand open, letting in a cool breeze and the sounds of the city below. Wyn flicks on an overhead chandelier.

We're in a bedroom, obviously, given the white-painted four-poster bed that dominates the room. The rest of the furniture matches the bed—a dressing table, nightstand, wardrobe—all in white with dainty hand-painted orange floral designs decorating their corners. The pale yellow coverlet on the bed matches the walls, and little embroidered pillows sit in a tidy row across the top of the bed. A small white cast-iron bistro table and chair sit on the balcony, which is laced with some kind of deep orange tropical flowers.

"So the portal is somewhere nearby, or are we just resting?" I ask, inspecting the photos and postcards tucked inside the frame of the dressing table's big oval mirror. The photos look like old movie star glamour shots, good-looking people from decades ago, their scrawled signatures across the bottom. The illustrated postcards say things like "Hello from Havana!" and feature smiling girls in flouncy dresses shaking maracas or holding up their skirts to show off long shapely legs. A hand mirror, a brush, and several little pots of makeup sit on the dressing table along with a few of those old glass perfume bottles with the attached spritzers.

In the mirror I can see Wyn standing rather awkwardly, his hands shoved in the front pockets of his jeans, a somewhat sheepish look on his face. That's when it dawns on me. This must be his girlfriend's room . . . his *virtual* girlfriend's room. Usually I would find this funny, but for some reason, I feel irritated. Really, really irritated.

"So . . . the portal?" I say, unable to keep the peevishness from my voice.

Wyn clears his throat. "It's through there," he says quietly, pointing his thumb toward the wardrobe.

"You're kidding me, right?"

Wyn shakes his head.

Now I laugh, enjoying the embarrassed smile that plays across his lips.

"Your portal is through the wardrobe. Wow, you've created your own little Narnia," I say, walking toward the large cupboard. "Does it come with a talking lion, too?" I pull open the wardrobe doors with both hands.

There's nothing there. And by nothing, I mean *really* nothing. No portal, no Landing, no fur coats leading to a snowy forest. Inside the wardrobe there's just . . .

Wait, is that . . . ?

"*Fy fæn*," I say, closing the doors as quickly as I can. I step away from the wardrobe without taking my eyes off it.

There *was* nothing there. Less than nothing. Only a pulsing, roiling, cavernous void. Yet it seemed to want to reach out. It seemed . . . *alive.*

I have never seen anything like it before. I didn't even believe it existed.

I glance at Wyn, but he doesn't need to say anything. Doesn't bother to explain. We both know exactly what I was staring into.

The Black.

No. I won't be scared. Because there's nothing to be afraid of. All those stories Chang tells about the Black are just that. Stories.

I think about opening the doors again. Just to prove to

myself it's no big deal, but I can't bring myself to do it. Frustration bubbles up inside me, a sudden surge of anger, and I try to push it back down.

"What?" Wyn asks.

"Where the hell did that come from?" I say.

"I told you. They took away the portal," Wyn states. "There's no way out."

"And by *they*, you mean . . . ?" I ask as I start shaking the wardrobe. Maybe it's just a glitch, some kind of malfunction. Maybe if I disrupt the code, the portal will snap back into place.

"I don't know, but someone's behind this, someone is deliberately trying to keep me from going home," he says, running a hand through his hair again. "Wait, what are you doing?"

"What does it look like I'm doing?" I pull the heavy wardrobe away from the wall so I can examine the back of it. Nothing there. I pound on the wall where the wardrobe was, then give it a good strong kick.

"Stop that," Wyn says, pulling on my arm. "You're ruining it."

The pale yellow wall now has a hole in it the size of my foot. I peer through, but there's nothing but Black on the other side. I jerk away from it, and swear again.

"Come on, we're leaving," Wyn says, pulling on my arm. I can tell he's upset that I'm messing with his girlfriend's prissy little room. "Your mind is on overload right now; you don't know what you're doing."

For some reason, his words just make me madder than ever. I yank my arm back. "I'm not done yet," I say. I stand behind the wardrobe and lean into it.

"Stop!" Wyn yells at me, but it's too late. The wardrobe teeters for a moment, then crashes into the four-poster bed. Both pieces of furniture collapse and splinter.

"Pretty shoddy workmanship," I quip to Wyn as I kick through the rubble.

"What the hell do you think you're doing?" Wyn asks me now, his eyes filled with anger, his voice rising.

"I'm trying to get us out of here, you spoiled brat," I say, irritated by his bossiness. *I'm* still the one in charge. *I'm* the person his father hired to find a way out of here, and I'm determined to do so.

"Don't worry," I continue, "I'm sure your virtual girlfriend won't mind a little redecorating." With that, I pick up the cast-iron chair from the balcony and start swinging it into the walls. Smashing things feels good, for some reason, like I'm somehow getting back at the MEEP for what it's put me through today. I let loose with the chair and rip the entire room to shreds. For a final touch, I throw the chair straight at the dressing table. It shatters the vanity mirror and the photos and postcards disappear under a mound of broken glass.

Wyn has been yelling at me to stop this whole time, but

I ignore him. It's just a stupid room, nothing he can't rebuild once I get us out of here. I start inspecting all the holes I've created, hoping one of them will lead to the portal.

Wyn's standing in the doorway, his fists clenched, his eyes blazing. "This is MY world, not yours. You have no right to destroy my creation."

"I'll do whatever I want," I say, the words shooting from my mouth like darts. "Your daddy's my boss, not you, remember?"

He looks furious now, but I don't care. It's like another Nixy has taken over my body, and I'm okay with that. The real Nixy can't handle any more.

"Just leave," he says, his voice low and growly. "The only way you can help me is to go back and explain what's happened to my father."

I turn around and examine another hole in the wall. Black. They're all filled with it. It undulates, shifts. I can sense it moving, more than see it. Its darkness is total and complete.

"All you're doing now is making it worse," Wyn says. "Go home, Nixy."

I kick another hole in the wall. "You know what? Fine. Inventory," I say, blinking as the sidebar comes up in my mind. I open the file that has my emergency code listed. "I'll go back home and draw a map for your daddy and his minions so they can come and find you. And then you can bitch to them about *their* rescue methods."

His face flashes something else now, something more sad than angry, and he opens his mouth as if to say something.

And then there is a sound. Or rather, a *change* in the sound. A dampening of it, like my ears popping in an elevator.

I turn and see the wall behind me begin to fuzz and break into fractals, like static on a TV. The surface bends crazily—the image of it stretching, twisting. I watch as the Black pulses out of the hole I've made. It swallows the wall in great, large sections.

It's mesmerizing. I can do nothing but stand and stare at the wall as this presence—this *thing*—devours it.

"Go," Wyn says.

I blink at him. The Black moves onto the floor, oozing, turning the surface I'm standing on into . . . nothing.

"GO!" he barks. He grabs my shoulder and steers me toward the door. Outside the room, he closes the door behind us, and locks it tight with a key from his pocket.

"Wh-what?" I sputter. "How? Are we—?"

Wyn presses his lips together. "I think it will stay contained inside the room," he tells me. "It never did . . . *that* before."

We stare at the wood frame. It holds fast—stable, solid.

Wyn turns to me. "I think . . . Nixy, I think you should go."

I blow out a long breath. I feel like I can barely think, much less *save* anybody. "Look, maybe the programmers can find a way to create a new portal for you, once I explain the problem."

He tries to smile at me, though he looks anything but happy. "Please tell my grandmother that I miss her and I'll be home as soon as I can."

I feel a twinge of guilt thinking of Mama Beti. How disappointed she'll be when I return empty-handed. But it can't be helped. Wyn's right. There's no easy escape and I've done my best.

I found Wyn. Now someone else needs to get him the hell out of here.

I nod a quick good-bye, then recite the eleven-number code into the MEEPosphere, waiting for the familiar beeping sound to take me back to reality.

I wait a little longer. No beeps. I'm still in the hallway of Wyn's imagined Cuban town house, and Wyn is starting to look worried.

I blink and look up the code again. Maybe I mixed up the numbers. I recite them again, this time more loudly. "5-1-1-9-6-1-0-0-7-0-0."

Nothing. Across from me I see Wyn's shoulders fall, his head drop. He raises his hands and massages his forehead with his fingertips.

I run down the stairs and out onto the cobbled street, yelling the numbers into the night sky. "5-1-1-9-6-1-0-0-7-0-0!"

Beside me a car honks.

A small group of Meeple hail a cab.

The code. It doesn't work.

I am trapped here . . . with Wyn.

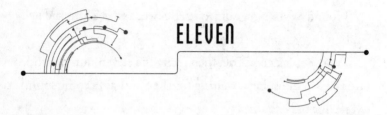

ELEVEN

MY HEAD IS POUNDING, LIKE THERE'S A CYMBAL-PLAYING MONKEY going to town inside my brain. I consider shooting it with my laser gun—that ought to shut it up—but something about that plan seems wrong. I'm too tired to figure out *what* though.

Why can't I think? I lean against the town house's exterior wall, then close my eyes and slide down it into a heap.

The monkey doesn't stop. *BANG BANG BANG BANG.* I tuck my head down and put my hands over my ears, which is useless, but I can't seem to do anything else.

After a few moments I register a hand on my knee and a soft voice saying, "Hey there."

The monkey does its best to drown out the voice. *BANG BANG BANG.*

"Nixy, can you hear me?" the voice says, more loudly this time.

I blink and try to pull myself together. I nod and then wince. Moving my head makes me dizzy.

"Come on, let's get out of here," Wyn says. He gently helps me to my feet. "You need to rest."

He takes my hand like I'm a five-year-old and leads me around the back of the house, where a motorcycle's been parked in the alley. He climbs on, then tells me to get on the back and hold tight. As we ride through the city, weaving around cars, we don't talk—I *can't* talk—and I'm glad Wyn doesn't ask me any questions. I have no answers right now. I can barely remember my own name. I just rest my head on his back and let him drive. The monkey cymbals are not as loud now.

We finally reach a huge, stately hotel, its majestic entrance framed with towering palm trees standing sentry. The sign on the door reads HOTEL NACIONAL. Wyn leaves the motorcycle with a uniformed valet, and we walk through a lush lobby, where more beautiful Meeple stand about talking and laughing and clinking little ice cubes in their drink glasses. Some of the people look familiar and I wonder if they are more famous movie stars—or the same famous movie stars. I open my mouth to ask Wyn, but nothing comes out.

Wyn squeezes my hand. "Don't worry, we're almost there." He leads me to an elevator, where another hotel attendant says, "Good evening, Mr. Salvador," and presses a button. The elevator goes up to the top of the hotel and lets us out into a luxurious hallway. A small voice in my head is trying to tell me something—warning me—something about strange boys and hotel rooms being a bad idea, but my hand, the one that is holding Wyn's, ignores that voice, and it soon goes away.

We go through a service door, up a flight of stairs, and Wyn opens a door into the night sky. We are on the roof of the hotel. He leads me to a small garden and pushes me gently into a wicker recliner. "Wait here," he says.

In the distance, I can make out the ocean, its waves slow and steady as they approach then retreat from the seawall surrounding the city. The sound is restful, hypnotic, and soon the cymbals in my head go away entirely. A handful of stars twinkle above me, like fairies. I feel as if I could almost fall asleep, which is ridiculous. I'm in the MEEP. Avatars don't sleep.

"Here you go," whispers Wyn. His arms are full of linens and pillows. He tucks a pillow under my head and covers me with a silky, lightweight blanket. As my eyelids flutter down for the last time, I see him settle into the recliner next to mine. He is staring up at the stars.

When I next open my eyes, there is a beautiful pink-and-orange haze surrounding me. I blink once, then burrow my head back into the pillow and reach for Hodee, who likes to sleep inside the nest of my curled body each night. Only he's not there. I register this as strange, but I'm not ready to fully wake up yet to investigate further. This pillow is so soft, the sound of the waves so soothing. . . .

Waves. Ocean? Something is wrong with that, I know. My brain is trying to pull itself out of slumber, but it's like it's fighting itself. Half of it is saying, "Ocean waves . . . mmm." The other half is saying, "Ocean waves . . . wha?"

The "wha" side wins.

I open my eyes. A gorgeous boy sits across from me, watching me. He smiles. "Go ahead and take a minute," he says.

I don't even need the full minute. Within seconds it all comes back to me like a full-scale tsunami: the sharks, the anaconda, the pterodactyls, the banshee, and of course, Wyn. I'm in the MEEP. Not only that, I'm a prisoner here.

I sit up slowly, combing my fingers through my hair and running my tongue over my teeth. I've never slept in the MEEP before; I feel like I should have rumpled clothes and morning breath. But when I glance down, my avatar looks as fresh as ever. That's a bonus.

"I don't get it," I say to Wyn, who's still watching me. "Why was I so tired? Avatars don't need to sleep."

"Avatars don't, but our brains do," says Wyn. He picks up the blanket on his chair and begins to fold it. "What's the longest you've ever played in the MEEP?"

I hesitate. I signed a MEEP contract promising I would always abide by the "4 hours per every 24 hours" maximum.

Wyn grins at me. "Be honest. I swear I won't tell my dad's legal department."

I grin back and shrug. "I don't know . . . maybe eight hours?"

"So compare that to the twenty-four hours you've been in the MEEP this time around."

"What?" I say, standing now. "I've been gone a *whole day*?"

"I think so, from what you've told me. That's why you were so exhausted last night. Even though your body is at rest at home, your brain keeps working here. And after all you'd been through yesterday—the maze challenges and, well, finding me—"

He pauses for a second, and I recall the raging hissy fit I threw yesterday, like I was somehow channeling King Kong. A wave of embarrassment runs all the way through me and I look away.

"Your brain was on overload," he continues. "It needed to shut down for a while—in the real world."

I guess it made sense. "I hadn't really thought of that before," I confess.

Wyn takes the blanket from my recliner and I grab the other end to help him fold it.

"I hadn't either," he says, "until I totally crashed on the beach one night and woke up the next morning eyeball-to-eyeball with a large crab."

I laugh as he takes the folded blanket from me and scoops up the pillows.

We leave the roof and go back into the hotel, stopping by one of the rooms to return the linens he'd pilfered the night before. The hotel room is decked out in swanky retro furniture and boasts a panoramic view of the ocean. "Did you really go to the trouble of building and furnishing every single room in this hotel?"

Wyn gives a small laugh. "It wasn't as hard as it sounds," he says, as he begins to make up the bed. I lean over to help him. I don't know whether to find it charming or crazy that he's so intent on keeping our MEEP prison nice and tidy. "All the rooms are identical, a simple copy-and-paste job," he continues. "Eventually I might re-create some of the penthouse suites, but it's not my top priority."

"I assume you mean the Let's-get-the-hell-out-of-here thing takes precedence?"

Wyn looks out the window and sighs. "Of course."

"I'm going to need to know everything," I say. "Why don't you start at the beginning?"

He nods. "Right. Let's go to the Malecón. We can talk there."

The Malecón, it turns out, is the big stone seawall that I saw last night from the rooftop. As we walk along the top of it, we see fishermen, townspeople, fruit vendors, and lovers holding hands. I suddenly remember Wyn holding my hand last night and I bite my lip, but Wyn doesn't seem to notice. He has turned inward, trying to figure out where to start his story.

"I've been working on this world for two years now," he says, looking out at the ocean as we walk. "I guess you could say it's my hobby, the one place I spend most of my time when I'm not at school."

"Two years." I nod in understanding. "When your dad invents the greatest video game of all time, you don't have to wait for the official release like the rest of us."

Wyn looks almost apologetic. "I know that seems unfair—" he starts, but I cut him off.

"I would have done the same thing. My dad's a developmental artist on the MEEP team. He lets me try new stuff all the time. Just not on a . . . scope of . . . this magnitude," I say, waving an arm at the miles-long stretch of Havana coastline.

"So that's why you're so good at this," Wyn says with a grin. "You inherited the video game gene from your father."

"Both my parents, really," I say, and all of a sudden I miss them horribly. "My mom, Jill, is a scriptwriter."

"Jill?" Wyn asks, stopping us in our tracks. "Jill Bauer?"

"You know her?" I ask, though I'm sure that can't be right. Jill would have told me if she'd ever met Diego Salvador's son.

"Well, I know *of* her. I use her scripts all the time. More than half the Meeple here in Havana speak JillBauer-ese," he says, laughing. "She's funny as hell, your mom. Always throws in some wacky surprise. Makes the Meeple more interesting."

I admit that I am a little taken aback, and also a little ashamed of myself. I have always thought of my dad's work on the MEEP as super creative and exciting, and my mom's work as . . . well, boring.

"So both your parents are in the biz," Wyn continues. "Is that why they named you Nixy . . . for the water sprite boss in *Sirens of the Seylon Sea*?"

"God, no!" I say, giving him a small swat on the arm. "But the truth is almost as fruity. My full name is Phoenix Ray Bauer. Phoenix for the mythological bird, Ray for Ray Bradbury, my mom's favorite author."

"Sounds like our moms are . . . *were* . . . the same kind of crazy. My full name is Elwyn Brooks Salvador."

"No idea who Elwyn Brooks is," I say. "Sorry."

Wyn laughs. "Don't worry, no one does. But I'm sure you've read *Charlotte's Web* by E. B. White?"

"Yes, and—?" I say, not quite following.

"Elwyn Brooks . . . E. B.?"

Now I am really laughing. "Wow, E. B., that is *almost* as embarrassing as my name."

"Well, my mom's maiden name was Brooks, so I give her a pass on that one. But the 'Elwyn' was certainly cruel and unusual punishment." He grumbles, though he is smiling. I remember the photo of his mother on the piano; he has that same warm smile that reaches the eyes.

"Maybe Elwyn is a little old-fashioned," I say, "but I give your mom an A-plus for originality. *Charlotte's Web* is one of my favorites. Besides, Wyn's a cool nickname. Like, *for the Wyn*!" I yell, raising my hand in the air for a high five.

Now he is shaking his head and laughing at me. "For the win!" he agrees, slapping my hand.

We walk in silence together for a few more moments, as if we're both trying to stretch this brief carefree interlude as long as we can.

"So when did things turn bad?" I finally ask. As much as I'm enjoying our walk, I know my parents must be truly worried by now. I've never taken this long on the job. "Here in the MEEP, I mean."

"Thanksgiving Day," he says. "I could tell right away that something was wrong. My usual frequency code sounded different, a pattern I didn't recognize. When I arrived at the Landing, I thought about stopping at the main control panel to make sure everything was all right, but the damn Christmas in the MEEP promotion started that day, and I just wanted to get the hell out of there."

I snort a little at that, and he raises his eyebrows at me.

"My dad was lead developer on Christmas in the MEEP," I explain.

"No offense to your dad," he hurries to explain. "It's *my* dad I was annoyed with. Christmas in the MEEP and this one-year anniversary have consumed him for months. We've hardly seen him. And once again, he bailed on my grandmother and me for Thanksgiving."

"I get it, believe me," I say, pushing my hair behind my ears as a breeze sweeps over us. "You should know, though, your dad feels bad about that."

Wyn shrugs and his face turns unreadable. "So anyway, I left the Landing in a hurry and walked through the portal. I came through the wardrobe, then immediately left the bedroom. I was heading down the stairs when I heard a noise."

He pauses and I look at him in question.

"An impossible noise," he says, looking out at the ocean again.

I continue to stare at him, trying to be patient. "What do you mean an *impossible* noise?" I finally say, unable to wait any longer.

He turns to face me again. "I heard someone open and shut the wardrobe door."

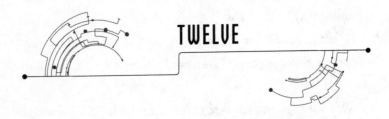

TWELVE

"ARE YOU SAYING THINGS TURNED BAD WHEN SOMEONE FOLLOWED you into the MEEP?" I ask Wyn, as we continue along the seawall. "Why? Anyone who has a beta code could have entered. I do it all the time in my line of work."

"Yes, but I have my own private frequency, Nixy. I coded it myself, with help from my father. We're the only two who know it. And I knew that *he* wasn't going to follow me . . . he was in California for the anniversary launch."

"So what did you do after you heard the noise?"

"I went back to the bedroom, but it was empty. And when I opened the wardrobe door, there was nothing but Black."

A small chill runs down my back, though the virtual Havana sunshine is perfect and the temperature warm. "Okay, what happened then?"

"Well," says Wyn, blowing out a slow breath from his cheeks, "I still wasn't *that* worried. I figured maybe it was just a technical glitch—maybe my ear trans needed replacing or the MEEP network was acting up. I use a lot of beta programming, so it wouldn't be too strange to run across a problem now and then."

I nod as he speaks, encouraging him to go on. It all sounds reasonable enough.

"So that's when I initiated my return frequency. Only it didn't work."

"Did you try yelling *really loudly*?" I ask with a rueful grin, remembering my ridiculous display last night.

Wyn smiles at me. "Believe me, I would have broken your eardrums if you'd been here. I think I tried about a half dozen times before I gave up. It's a panicky feeling," he says, as if letting me know that my temper tantrum last night wasn't completely uncalled-for. "I spent the next twenty-four hours running all over the place, trying every door, yelling random codes, killing myself over and over . . . that's how I ended up falling asleep on the beach, in fact. I'd just taken a running swan dive off the seawall, hoping I'd break my neck and reanimate in the Landing."

"And instead you took a cozy nap with crab daddy," I say, peering down at the beach below, though there isn't much of it left. The tide is rolling in fast now. "Surprised you didn't drown."

Wyn stops and looks over the seawall with me. "I've been fooling around with the tides, trying to create a schedule for them that mimics the real tide charts of Havana. It's almost high tide now. In fact, we'd better turn around and make our way back if we don't want to get splashed. The bigger waves come right over the wall."

"So back to your story," I say as we reverse our tracks. In the distance I can see the towering white Hotel Nacional gleaming in the morning sun. It looks like a palace. "What happened after you woke up on the beach?"

Wyn shrugs. "I tried to keep calm. I figured my grandmother would be the first to notice I'd been gone too long. I knew she'd be worried and probably call my father, and that my father would send in one of his programmers to fix the problem."

"So you also thought it was a technical issue," I say. "But yesterday you told me that someone was intentionally keeping you trapped here?"

Wyn's face turns dark and he shoves his hands into his pockets. "We're not the only people here, Nixy."

"What? How do you know?" I ask, eyeing the Meeple around us.

He shrugs. "The subtle differences that come from a lack of script. Small idiosyncrasies. I don't have to tell you about them. You just know, don't you?"

I nod because I do. I've always been able to sense my marks, even when they're surrounded by Meeple. But I also knew exactly what I was looking for. *Who* I was looking for. "Have you spoken to them?"

Wyn shakes his head. "No, they've been successfully avoiding me. They try to blend in with the crowd, but I programmed this entire world from scratch . . . and they just don't fit in."

"Have you tried chasing them down, capturing them?"

"Of course. I thought maybe you were one of them yesterday, that's why I—"

"Mugged me?"

"Sorry," he says, the sheepish grin back on his face. "They always get away from me, initiating their return frequencies before I can even talk to them. So I guess you could say I was trying a more . . . forceful technique."

"Yes, I *could* say." I swat him again on the arm to let him know I'm kidding. Then I silently chastise myself for reverting to first grade. Why do I keep hitting him?

"Did you ever consider that shooting me yesterday might simply have reset me back to the Landing?"

Wyn nods. "It was a risk, but I had nothing to lose. I figured if I couldn't shoot myself back home, maybe no one else could get back that way either. Besides, I wasn't really going to aim at your head. I figured I'd just pop you in the leg and maim you if you got out of hand."

I bite my lip, but I know I'm smiling anyway. "So where do these non-Meeple people usually hang out?" I ask, tucking my hands under my arms to keep them from touching him.

Wyn gives me a sideways look. "Usually they just follow me."

I stop then and whip my head around. If these *rasshøls* are the ones responsible for this mess, I've got a few choice words for them. After I knock their teeth out, of course.

"How can we draw them out from the—?" I start, but just then something lurches beneath my feet and I nearly fall into Wyn. The stone seawall begins to buck and tremble like we've been hit by a magnitude seven earthquake. Wyn grabs my arms and tries to steady me, though it doesn't do much good. We're both flailing around like first-timers trying to couples skate at the roller rink.

"Don't be—" Wyn yells, but he's cut off by a deafening roar.

"BRRRAAAAAOOOKKKK!"

A piercing squawk bellows from the sea. A huge, slimy, saucer-eyed head emerges from the water, its gaping beak lined with a thousand dagger-like teeth. The beast rises higher and higher, lifting four huge flailing tentacles out of the water. It doesn't take a genius to know it's got four more where those came from. A freaking *kraken* has just come to call on Havana.

"BRRRAAAAAOOOKKKK!" it screams again, then charges the seawall.

"Nixy—" Wyn yells, but before he can go on, the kraken extends a hoary purple tentacle and snatches Wyn right off the wall.

Oh my God, oh my God, oh my God is all that goes through my head.

Finally, I snap my gaping mouth shut and yell, "Inventory!" I have no idea what to use against a kraken. Laser gun? Crossbow? The monster's skin looks to be made of hard scales, completely impenetrable.

Wyn is still screaming at me, though I can't make out the words. The kraken starts to bring Wyn toward its toothy beak. "*Fy fæn*," I mutter, then load the crossbow and take aim. I try to zero in on one of its milky eyes, though the beast keeps moving, making it nearly impossible to target. "Steady," I tell myself, finger on the trigger. My crosshatch finds a big liquid pupil, and I start to squeeze.

"Nooooooo," yells Wyn.

No what? I've lost the shot now. What is he screaming about?

"Nixy, don't shoot," he yells again.

What? I lower the crossbow in disbelief. It looks like the kraken is . . . hugging Wyn to his cheek? Wyn strokes him and says something over and over again . . . something that sounds suspiciously like "Good boy. There's a good boy."

Finally, the kraken paddles over to where I'm standing and

gently replaces Wyn on the seawall. Wyn gives me a goofy grin.

I am not amused.

"What the hell is *that*?" I ask, pointing my loaded crossbow at the kraken. The beast is now bobbing in the water next to us, waving its tentacles around like it wants to play.

"That's Larry. Watch this," he says, summoning a nearby fruit vendor with a whistle. Wyn quickly buys a bunch of bananas, then winds up and starts pitching them one by one at the kraken.

I have to admit, Larry's a pretty good outfielder. When he's caught a banana in each tentacle, he does what can only be described as a little happy dance—a few giddy spins, a couple of head bobs—then waves to us in farewell before sinking back into the deep.

"You've got to be kidding," I say. "And here I've been admiring your devotion to historical accuracy, when all this time you've had a pet kraken floating around?"

Wyn laughs. "Sorry I forgot to warn you about him. Every now and then I get a bit bored trying to re-create the real Havana, so I throw in a few extras to amuse myself."

"I see. Any other . . . *extras* I should know about before I kill them by mistake?"

Wyn grins. "None as alarming as Larry. I'll try to give you a heads-up next time."

"I would appreciate that. Now let's figure out a way to

ambush those intruders. I have a few tricks up my sleeve that may help."

"Tricks up your sleeve? Oh, don't you sound like Nancy Drew," Wyn teases, his eyes twinkling.

I resist the urge to swat his arm again. "Just take me somewhere we can make a plan—someplace we won't find any Meeple, or hideous sea monsters who think they're golden retrievers."

"I know just the place. This way," he says, and holds out his hand to me.

The hand flusters me. I want to take it, but I'm also embarrassed by it. He's already saved me from careening off the seawall during the Larry episode. I don't want him to think I'm some little girl who can't take care of herself.

I fought sharks to get here, damn it. *I'm* the rescuer, not him.

I pretend I don't notice the hand. "Lead on," I say.

He quickly drops his hand and turns his head. He shoves his fists into his pockets and starts walking briskly away from me. Great. Maybe we should both go back to first grade.

Neither of us talks as we head back down the busy Havana streets. There are Meeple everywhere. At first I try to scrutinize everyone within eyesight, but Wyn is walking too fast, and besides, I don't know what I'm looking for.

Finally, we turn down a residential street that looks familiar, only in the daytime it's even prettier. I wish the houses back in Illinois were this colorful.

"You're taking me back to the wardrobe house?" I ask, when I finally catch up to Wyn at the doorway. I'm relieved to see it hasn't been absorbed by the hideous Blob I released last night, though I'm still not sure we should go back in.

"It's the one place I know we'll be alone," he says. "Don't worry, we won't go upstairs," he adds, guessing my thoughts. The warmth has gone out of his eyes and voice, but he is still kind, still polite as he enters the house first. "It's the only building in Havana where Meeple aren't allowed."

I think of the girl's bedroom upstairs, the one I've destroyed. The one I thought belonged to some virtual girlfriend.

Only Meeple aren't allowed inside this house.

"Oh," I say, unable to suppress the surprise in my voice.

He glances at me as we walk through the first floor of the house. "I thought you'd have it all figured out by now, Nancy Drew."

I try not to get riled by the sarcasm in his voice.

We enter a walled patio at the back of the house. The white-washed stone walls are covered with greenery and flowers, and a water fountain burbles in the middle of a small sitting area. Wyn gestures for me to have a seat on one of the iron benches.

"This is a replica of my grandmother's old house," he says quietly, sitting on the next bench over.

"Mama Beti's?"

Wyn nods. "She and her family left Havana just before the Revolution in '59. Mama Beti was fifteen. They had to leave everything behind. And then they never got to go back."

Shame washes over me. "That was her bedroom," I say. I don't have to ask, I know I'm right.

"Yes."

"Has she been here yet? Has she seen it?"

Wyn shakes his head. "Not yet. She hasn't had the frequency procedure."

I look down at the ground, unable to look him in the eye. I am an idiot. "I'll help you rebuild her room, Wyn, as soon as we get out of here. I promise."

"It's okay, the repairs shouldn't be too difficult once we're out," he says, looking down at his hands. "Besides, it's not an *exact* replica. I don't have much to work with other than Mama Beti's memories and a few old photographs."

"Does she know you're doing this?"

"She knows I'm up to something because I ask her questions constantly. But I still think she'll be surprised. I hope she likes it."

I stare into his eyes, hoping to relay the depth of my words. "It's beautiful here, Wyn. How could she not be thrilled to see her childhood home again?" I stop then, remembering Mama Beti's metal walker. "How will that work? I thought only healthy people could get the MEEP piercing . . . heck, there are kids at my school who aren't allowed to get pierced because they're on allergy medication."

Wyn smiles, and I'm glad to see his face look happy again. "That's the truly amazing part. My father has some medical scientists in Belgium working on a special frequency for her. If all goes well, she'll be one of the first disabled people to 'walk' in the MEEP. And it's not just Mama Beti . . . these researchers are working on technologies that would eventually allow people with all sorts of physical limitations to experience a healthy body in the MEEP. Not only will the lame be able to walk, but the blind will be able to see. Old people can feel young again."

"Wow," I say, sitting back onto the bench. "I had no idea your dad was involved in *that* kind of research."

"He keeps it all pretty top secret . . . doesn't want to let the cat out of the bag until all the tests have been done, all the questions answered."

I'm stunned. Maybe Diego Salvador isn't such a bad guy after all. "And here I thought the MEEP was just one big money grab . . . no offense."

"Actually, my father spends a lot of his profits from the gaming side of the MEEP on private medical research. When you think about all the diseases and disabilities out there . . . virtual reality could relieve the suffering of millions, maybe billions of people on this planet."

Wyn is more animated than I've ever seen him, now that he's warmed to his topic. And I have to admit, I'm pretty blown away by this news—the idea that the MEEP can be more than just a virtual rec center for bored teens.

"I mean, think of all the educational opportunities out there, especially once the multiplayer capabilities are released to the public," he continues. "Imagine the virtual museums that historians could create. Teachers could take their students on field trips to ancient Egypt or Machu Picchu during the height of the Incan empire . . . professors could lecture inside the Parthenon in Athens or the Colosseum in Rome."

"English majors could drink daiquiris with Ernest Hemingway in Havana," I chime in, remembering my new friends at the Floridita.

"Exactly," he says, laughing. "MeaParadisus can be so much more than a gaming platform. It could change the world as we know it, use our brains in ways that will enhance life and broaden our knowledge."

I get up from my bench and go sit next to him. "That's truly incredible, Wyn," I say, taking his hand, and I mean it.

I hold my breath for a minute, hoping he doesn't pull away. I can't blame him if he does; I've had my claws out ever since I got here.

He looks down at my hand and squeezes it, then smiles at me. "You're pretty incredible yourself, Nixy Bauer."

I can't help it.

I melt into those chocolate eyes like marshmallows in cocoa.

I know, I know.

I need to get out of here.

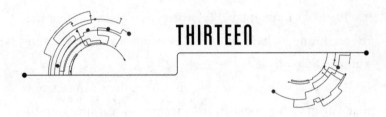

THIRTEEN

THE TROPICANA IS HOPPING. HUNDREDS OF MEEPLE ARE DINING, dancing, gambling, and mingling in the various rooms of the enormous nightclub. Wyn is giving me the full tour, and I'm truly amazed at how much work he's put into this place. The men are all in trim suits and tuxedos, hair slicked back and shoes just as shiny, but it's the women who truly stand out in their glamorous evening gowns, jewels, and beauty shop updos. I've put on my wench dress for the occasion. I stick out like a sore thumb, but the Meeple don't notice, and Wyn seems to like it because he keeps, shall we say, *not meeting my eyes.*

The meadow-green aproned dress *is* cut pretty low and the laced bodice makes me look curvier than usual.

"Stop it!" I say, laughing as he pretends to sneak a peek at my cleavage. "For all you know, these are just enhancements."

That startles him.

"I . . . I've never thought about your avatar being enhanced. Is it?"

He looks more than a little perplexed by the notion that the real me might look different. "Does it matter?" I say, teasing him, but only a little.

"No, of course not," he says, his voice earnest. "In fact, now that I'm thinking about it, if I met you in real life, I probably couldn't handle it. I'd faint or hyperventilate. Because I'm suave like that. Truly, I hope you *are* enhanced, for the sake of all humanity."

"Good answer," I say, grinning like a fool. I can't help it. He's kind of perfect right now. Except for the sexy cigarette girl coming toward us, her eyes glued to Wyn, her big red lips smiling seductively.

She's wearing little more than a gold-sequined, strapless bathing suit, matching high heels that make her bronzed legs look a mile long, and some heavy-duty cleavage that takes mine right out of the race.

"Wyn, *amorcito*!" she says, turning her tray of cigarettes to the side so she can lean over and kiss Wyn on both cheeks.

Wyn looks over at me with a grin and I narrow my eyes at him.

"Nixy, meet Guadalupe," he says, looking more amused than he should be.

"Call me Lupe," she says, smiling at me. "Nice to meet you, *princesa*. Care for a cigarillo? On the house for a pretty girl like you."

"No thanks, Loopy," I say, looking pointedly at Wyn. He rewards me with a small laugh.

"How about a nice Cuban fatty then," Lupe says, picking up a huge cigar, "to put a little hair on your chest, *princesa*."

My mouth drops open and Wyn cracks up.

"I don't think so," I say, placing a hand over my chest, as if to protect it from Lupe's cigar voodoo.

"I know, I give you a *Romeo y Julieta*," says Lupe, handing me a smaller, single wrapped cigar and a box of matches. "You young lovers can take turns puffing on it," she says with a sly look at me and a wink at Wyn.

"*Gracias*, Lupe," Wyn says, "we'll do that."

"*Hasta la vista*, babydolls!" Lupe calls out with another flirty wink, then turns on her heel and walks away, her hips moving back and forth like a metronome.

"Wowza," I say, holding the cigar up. "Do you program all your Meeple ladies to be huge flirts, or just Loopy?"

Wyn laughs. "Just Lupe. She's Chucho's girlfriend . . . or she was Chucho's girlfriend, back in the real Havana."

"Chucho is . . . *was* Mama Beti's older brother, I'm guessing?"

"Yep. She's told me lots of great stories about him . . . he knew everybody who was anybody in Havana from working the bar at Floridita. So did Lupe. She used to sneak Mama Beti into the shows here at the Tropicana. Mama Beti told me that the real Lupe had kind of a, um . . . naughty sense of humor, I guess you could say."

"She'd make a sailor blush!"

"Latin Vixen IV script, courtesy of Jill Bauer," Wyn says, enjoying the look of horror that crosses my face.

"My *mom* wrote those lines?"

"For the most part. I just customized them a bit."

I shake my head. I need to have a little talk with Jill when I get home. *Nice Cuban fatty? Hair on your chest?* Honestly.

Wyn offers me his elbow. "Shall we dance now, *princesa*?"

I make a face. "If you're sure about this." I tuck the cigar and matches into the pocket of my wench apron and reluctantly take his arm.

"Trust me," he says, then leads me through the busy casino and through a set of glass doors.

We're in an outdoor ballroom now that Wyn tells me is called *Bajo las Estrellas* cabaret, which means "Under the Stars." And the place lives up to its name. The vast enclosure has been draped with a thousand strands of twinkly lights, making me feel like I'm in a fairy garden, only a tropical fairy garden with towering palm trees and a cigar-smoke haze. All the Meeple here look like movie stars at their candlelit tables, while a bevy of waiters and busboys and more scantily clad cigarette girls circulate among them.

Wyn had decided earlier that our best chance of finding any human players in the MEEP would be to go to the most crowded spot in Havana. It seemed counterintuitive to me at first, but he had insisted it would be the only way to lure them out. The only times he'd ever seen them, they'd been "hiding" in a crowd of Meeple.

An enormous stage at the end of the outdoor ballroom features a ten-piece band and a female singer who reminds me of Lupe: brassy, voluptuous, and . . . what word did Wyn use? Oh yeah. *Naughty.* But wow, can she sing. Her voice weaves in and out of the instruments playing behind her, the trumpets, piano, maracas, and bongo drums all just a showcase for her resonant voice and fiery presence.

"*AZUCAR!*" she yells, and some of the Meeple hoot and whistle in response.

Wyn pulls me onto the platform dance floor. I'm still not sure I want to do this.

"Can't we just sit at one of the tables and smoke our cigar?" I say, looking around at the other dancers. They're all moving in perfect time to the fast-paced music. I know they're programmed to do so, but still I feel intimidated.

"Smoking is bad for you. Just follow my lead," says Wyn, putting his right hand on my waist and taking my hand in his left. I feel slightly better now that he's holding on to me. Maybe he can just push me around the dance floor like a vacuum cleaner.

"They're playing a cha-cha now, easy as walking," he explains. "Here, watch my feet. One, two, cha-cha-cha, three, four, cha-cha-cha."

I do my best to imitate his steps. "One, two, cha-cha-cha," I repeat, "three, four, cha-cha . . . oops! Sorry about that."

We shuffle around like this several times, Wyn patiently counting out the steps with me. Not that it matters. I am a complete disaster at the cha-cha.

We try a mambo next, which is even worse.

"Okay!" says Wyn, after I've stepped on his foot for the twenty-seventh time. "Let's just stick to a simple two-step from now on. One-two, one-two, one-two," he counts.

This is more like it.

I look at the mambo-ing, salsa-ing, cha-cha-ing Meeple doing their complicated dance moves nearby. "Show-offs," I say, as Wyn and I two-step like hillbillies around the dance floor.

"They got nothing on us," Wyn says, putting his hands around my waist and lifting me into the air. As we twirl around I stretch my arms out like a ballerina. "Thatta girl, *princesa*!" he says, laughing at my dramatic pose.

I love hearing him laugh. I almost wish we didn't have work to do.

But now that I don't have to worry so much about my feet, I start scoping the place as we circle through the room. "I recognize Frank Sinatra," I say. "But point out the rest of the famous people to me."

As we circuit the dance floor, Wyn shows me all the custom Meeple he's programmed based on the prestigious guest list of the Tropicana, back when it was the favorite playground of the rich and famous. I recognize many of the names—Marlon Brando, Nat King Cole, Sammy Davis Jr., Joan Crawford, and Elizabeth Taylor—but there are others he has to explain to me, like Edith Piaf, a French singer whose long, skinny eyebrows look like they've been applied with a Sharpie, and Rocky Marciano, a heavyweight boxer whose nose looks like it lost a fight with a bowling ball.

"See that woman over there in the long white dress with the short dark hair?" he asks, tilting his head at a corner of the room.

I look in that direction and spot her. The white satin of her dress clings to every curve of her body and her hair has been slicked against her head like a cap, with little ringlets framing her tawny face. Huge spirals of diamonds hang from her ears, as big as Christmas ornaments. She's gorgeous.

"Let me guess . . . another actress? Singer? Dancer?"

"All of the above," he answers. "That's Josephine Baker. She was quite the sensation back in the day."

"Who's the Rico Suave with her?" I ask, thinking the tall, dark, tuxedoed man sitting across from her is pretty sensational as well. He is drinking from a martini glass and giving Josephine a smoky look across the table.

Wyn shrugs. "No one famous, just one of the stock Meeple. Latin Lover III, I think."

"Oooh, he sounds like fun," I say, wondering if Jill has given him a bunch of total cheeseball lines. I certainly hope so.

We continue to wing our way around the floor, watching for anything out of the ordinary, anything human among the Meeple.

"They're probably not on the dance floor," Wyn says. "Unless they're great dancers, this would be an easy place to give yourself away."

"You don't say?" I tease, and he lowers me into a dip like I'm Ginger Rogers. I kick up a leg for flourish and my long wench dress slides down to my thigh.

Wyn whistles at my bare leg and wags his eyebrows at me. "That leg must be enhanced, 'cause they don't make 'em that shapely in the real world."

"Steal that line from Latin Lover III?" I ask, as he pulls me back up.

He puts both arms around me now, like we're slow dancing, though the music is still loud and lively. We stay this way for a while, and I rest my head on his shoulder as I scan the tables again. Wyn's right: if there are any human players here, they would most likely be seated, where their nonautomated movements won't give them away.

So far, everyone just looks happy and fabulous. Marlon Brando is smoking a cigar and eyeing a cigarette girl. Nat King Cole and Sammy Davis Jr. are chuckling together and clinking glasses. Elizabeth Taylor is whispering something in Joan Crawford's ear. Joan Crawford looks unamused. Josephine Baker is adjusting her dangling earrings in a small compact while Rico Suave taps his foot impatiently. My eyes continue their search, though I'm starting to doubt this plan is working. I'm pretty sure the only two humans in this room are me and Wyn, and honestly, that's fine by me. I'm having fun and I don't want this night to—

"They're here," I say, jerking my head up as the realization finally dawns on me.

"Easy," Wyn says, continuing to dance. "Don't let them know you know. Tell me where they are, but smile like you're telling me what a great dancer I am."

"Josephine and Rico Suave," I say through my smile. "She had on spiral earrings before, not dangly ones. And he's tapping his foot out of sync with the music."

Wyn spins me around a bit so he can take a peek. "You're right. Ready for phase two?"

"Ready," I say, mentally rehearsing the next part of the plan.

"Okay, but you just put on your 'Nixy Bauer, Butt-kicker' face, which isn't going to work," he says, tapping me playfully on the nose. "We're supposed to be crazy about each other, remember?"

Oh yeah. I plaster a smile back on my lips, and tap his nose back in return. "Sorry, sweetcakes, guess I'm better at butt-kicking than acting."

"Don't worry, you'll get your chance," Wyn says, "but for now just pretend you're trying to woo me with your wenchi-ness."

I want to snort, but I titter instead behind a demure hand. Someone should award me an Oscar for this performance.

Wyn waits for the song to die down, then he leads me off the dance floor, right past their table. He puts his arm around me and kisses me on the cheek. "Thanks for one last dance, beautiful," he says, loud enough for them to hear. "Now let's blast through that alt portal and get home so I can kiss you in the real world."

I smile up at him like I'm head over heels in love with him, which isn't actually that hard, as it turns out, and we stroll out of the cabaret and into the casino. We pass the slot machines and roulette tables toward the staff door at the back of the room. About halfway through the casino, I throw my head back and pretend to laugh at something Wyn says. He picks me up and swings me around, like we're completely smitten with each other. While I'm swinging, I take a quick glance around the room.

"They took the bait," I whisper in his ear. "They're at the blackjack table directly behind us."

"Right. Let's do this," he says, then pushes through the door.

I open my inventory and equip the rappelling gun.

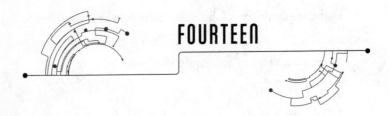

FOURTEEN

I CRASH DOWN ON JOSEPHINE LIKE A TON OF BRICKS AND SLAP MY hand over her mouth.

Wyn, whose job was to ambush Rico, swears, then looks out the staff door. It appears Rico sent Josephine in alone, the coward.

"Damn," Wyn says. "He's already vanished."

"That's okay, we still have Josie here," I say, looking down at my captive.

Josephine struggles frantically beneath me and I almost feel sorry for her. She never even saw me coming as I slid down the rappelling line and knocked her to the floor. Now I've got her pinned underneath me, though I've made one crucial mistake. I'm still in the wench dress, which makes it hard to maneuver.

"Closet!" I say, then quickly select my commando clothes. My avatar's outfit transforms instantaneously.

That's better. Now it's Josephine's turn.

"I want to see the real you," I say into the MEEPosphere without taking my eyes off Josephine. Her tawny skin, black hair, and white dress begin to pixelate like she's a human blender just switched to puree. A new image solidifies before us.

Holy heck.

"Kora?" Wyn and I both say at once.

Yes, Kora. Josephine Baker in her slinky satin dress has just transformed into Diego Salvador's trusted assistant. She's in a black catsuit, her long black hair pulled back into a no-nonsense ponytail. She wears no makeup, but her fingernails are long, sharp, and red. She looks ready to scratch my eyes out, but I've got her claws trapped firmly under my knees.

"What are you doing here? Did my father send you? Why didn't you reveal yourself?" Wyn asks in a tirade of questions, but I keep my hand clamped tightly over her mouth. "Let her speak, Nixy," he says. "Kora works for my dad. I've known her for years. She's here to help."

"I know who she is, but she's not *here to help*." I lean in, pinning her down harder. "Don't you get it? She's one of the bad guys."

Wyn shakes his head like he doesn't believe me. "She can't be. Kora's like family. . . . My dad trusts her implicitly."

Well, that was a huge mistake, I think, though I refrain from saying so out loud. The last thing I want to do is argue with Wyn. We've got bigger fish to fry.

Meanwhile, Kora is blinking rapidly, like she's trying to figure out what her story will be if I ever let her speak. She looks scared.

"If Kora came to rescue you," I say, "why was she stalking you in disguise? It makes no sense."

Wyn shrugs and looks at Kora for an answer. She turns her eyes away.

"You know I'm right," I tell him, wishing I was wrong.

Wyn still looks doubtful. "Kora," he says quietly, and her eyes turn back to his. "What are you doing here? Did my father send you?" he asks, then puts a hand on my shoulder. "Nixy, let her answer. If she starts reciting code or accessing her inventory you can stop her."

I purse my lips and give Kora my don't-even-think-about-it glare. "Fine. But she doesn't move." Slowly, I slide my hand off her mouth and put it around her neck instead.

"Let me go, please," she begs, her eyes looking at Wyn, not me. "I have to get back immediately. You don't understand."

"You're right, I don't understand," says Wyn, his eyes growing darker. "Enlighten me, Kora. Why have I been trapped here? What do you know?"

Kora's eyes dart between me and Wyn. "I can't say. Please,

let me go! If I'm not back soon, they'll kill me!"

"Who, my father?" exclaims Wyn. "Kora, what are you talking about?"

"Not your father, the . . . others," she says. "I told you, I can't say. But if they find out I've been caught, I don't know what they'll do."

I want to shake her now. "What *who* will do? Who are they? And why are they keeping us locked up here?"

Kora ignores me and keeps her gaze on Wyn. "Listen, just let me out of here and I'll go straight to your father, I promise. I'll tell him everything. It's the only way to save us both now. Wyn, please. Hurry!"

"Save us *both*?" I ask, glaring at Kora. "There are *three* of us here, by the way, and I'm not buying your little sob story. Now tell us how to get home."

Kora glares back at me, but I don't flinch. I've already won a staring contest with the Wicked Witch of the MEEP and Kora's got nothing on that hag.

She finally looks away and I glance at Wyn, who rubs a hand over his face. I can tell he's torn.

"She's bluffing, Wyn," I say, pressing down harder on Kora's shoulders with my knees. "I bet she's some corporate spy, paid to steal programming from your father. There's no way she's going to make nice with your dad at this point. It's too late; she's already incriminated herself. All she can do now is run and hope she's not caught. Right, Kora?"

Kora doesn't answer. Her eyes are wide and unblinking now, staring at the ceiling.

"Look, I don't know who or what you've got yourself messed up with, but just tell us how to get out of here," says Wyn, kneeling beside her. "You must know a way out. As soon as you tell us, we'll let you go."

I give Wyn a glare. I have no intention of letting Kora go so easily.

Then again, maybe it can't hurt to let her *think* we'll let her go.

"Wyn's right. We'll settle the rest of this when we get back. Just tell us how to return to the Landing and we'll all go home."

Kora doesn't answer at first, then suddenly yells, "8-9-7-4-5—"

I slap my hand over her mouth.

"Nice try," I say. I am losing patience with Wyn's good-cop tactics. Time for some bad cop. I need to get Kora to talk.

"Tell us how to get out of here, Kora, before your Big Boss decides this game is over," I say. "Who are you working for anyway? Russia? China? I bet those guys don't mess around. No wonder you're scared."

Kora narrows her eyes at me like I'm a fool, but I can see fear beneath the contempt.

"Tell us this minute, Kora, or I will tie you to the seawall and let the crabs pick at your eyeballs until you talk!" I say, getting right in her face. I slide my hand off her mouth but keep it raised only a few inches away, ready to slap it down at any second.

"Wyn, please—" she says again, looking over my shoulder.

Wyn begins to speak but I throw him a look and he swallows his words.

Kora's really starting to look scared now. "Okay, I'll tell you," she says, her voice trembling. "I'll tell you what I know, but then promise me you'll let me go before they find me."

Wyn nods.

"Start talking," I order.

"I work for LEGION. They've trapped Wyn here to blackmail Diego. They want him to give up control of the MEEP."

Wyn and I glance at each other. He looks as incredulous as I feel.

"LEGION?" he asks.

"That's ridiculous," I say. "LEGION's just a group of internet nerds with an axe to grind. They're hackers, not kidnappers. She's lying."

"It's the truth," Kora cries. "The LEGION you know—the amateur hackers and gamers—they're just a front, a source of data for the Legionnaires."

"Who?" I ask, my mind going a hundred miles a minute.

"The Legionnaires," she repeats. "I don't know their real

names or what they look like—no one does. But they've sworn to use any means necessary to bring down the MEEP."

"But why would they do that?" Wyn asks. "Kora, you know what the MEEP can do, what it can be . . . once my dad and his scientists work out the glitches, it could change the world!"

Kora's eyes fill with a mixture of pity and sadness now as she answers Wyn. "All your father has done, Wyn, is invent a form of mind control . . . mental slavery disguised as a game. Don't you see? Diego Salvador is the world's new Oppenheimer, only instead of creating an atomic bomb, he's created something even worse, something even more dangerous. One day your father's toy will control us, or kill us all."

Wyn is shaking his head, his eyes wild with disbelief. "That's a lie! You can't believe that!"

"I'm sorry, I never thought it would come to this," Kora continues, the pity in her eyes now replaced by tears. "I never thought you'd get hurt. I just wanted to stop your father. Now please, let me go! They'll be coming!" Her voice is almost a sob now and her whole body is shaking beneath me. "8-9-7—"

I slap my hand back over her mouth.

"Nixy—" Wyn starts, but I don't let him finish.

"We're not done yet. How do we get to the Landing, Kora? Where'd you hide the portal?"

Kora opens and closes her mouth a few times, like a fish. Her eyes stare straight up, almost glassy looking. She looks like she's about to have a seizure, but that's impossible. She's an avatar. Maybe she's bluffing, trying to throw us off balance so she can blurt out the numbers.

"Where's the portal, Kora?"

"Please," she says in a strangled gasp. "They're hurting me."

"Nixy, stop!" Wyn says, taking Kora's face between his hands. "Kora, are you okay? What's happening to you?"

Kora's body takes on a shimmery quality, like it might disappear any moment. We don't have time for this. I shove Wyn away from her. "The portal, Kora," I yell, my face just inches above hers. "Where is it?"

Her eyes roll a bit, but then they find me and she looks straight at me.

"Black," she whispers, as her body convulses once, then fades beneath me.

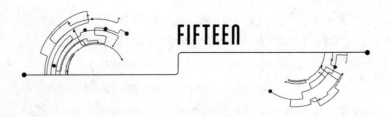

FIFTEEN

"WE'LL THINK MORE CLEARLY ONCE WE'VE HAD SOME SLEEP," WYN says, squeezing my hand.

We are walking through the lobby of the Hotel Nacional again. I'm a little more alert than I was last night when we were here, though equally distraught. I admit, I had a good cry in the Tropicana dressing room after Kora disappeared. I'm not sure exactly what happened to her, but there's a pretty good chance she wasn't lying. Which means there is a pretty good chance she's hurt, maybe even dead, and it's my fault.

I'm also pretty sure that if we *are* up against stone-cold killers, we are never getting back home.

As we go up in the elevator, I feel Wyn's eyes on me, deliberating, trying to decide what to do with me next. I don't blame him. I'm a bundle of raw feelings and my brain's on overdrive. Part of me feels like knocking down a few walls again to relieve my frustration. The other part of me wants to pull a Rip Van Winkle and sleep for the next hundred years.

"It's not your fault, you know," he says quietly.

"I trapped her here while someone in the real world was killing her," I finally say, as the elevator doors open.

"We don't know what truly happened, Nixy. Maybe she's still alive," Wyn says, but I can tell by his voice he doesn't believe it. Neither do I. We both felt the presence of death in that dressing room, something permanent when Kora's body disappeared. Besides, she never activated her return frequency code. And she'd been terrified. Which means either someone summoned her back remotely, or . . . she really died.

We stop by one of the hotel rooms to get blankets and pillows, and head to the rooftop.

"You know we don't have time for this," I say as Wyn pulls two recliners side by side and faces them toward the west.

"There's nothing else we can do right now, Nixy, so we might as well do something useful. Our brains need rest. And besides, look over there," he says, lowering himself into a recliner and pulling me down beside him.

The setting sun has made a picture in the sky, striping the horizon like a silk scarf of delicious colors: lemon meringue, orange sherbet, tangerine, blood orange, and pomegranate.

Wyn pulls a blanket over us and we lie there for a while in silence. I try to focus on the beauty of the sunset and let myself relax. Wyn is right, of course. Our plan to turn the tables on our captors failed miserably and now we have to think of a new one. Only I'm too tired. Too worried.

I think of my mom then with a small pang. I remember when I was younger, I was a total worrywart over every little thing. Jill would always tell me the best way to solve a problem was to sleep on it. "We work a lot of things out in our sleep," she would say, tucking me under the covers. "Sleep is the brain's night shift, and we'd best let it do its job." I used to imagine that my own brain's night crew was a bunch of sudsy bubbles, scouring my brain of all the bad, troublesome thoughts so I'd have a nice, clean, worry-free brain the next morning. Maybe I can summon the bubbles tonight.

I take a quick peek at Wyn. He is staring into the sunset, his face solemn and still, his mouth slightly turned down at the corners.

He turns to look at me. "Think you can sleep for a bit?" he asks, taking my hand in his.

"Sure," I say, squeezing his hand in return.

But before I close my eyes, I lean toward him. At the exact same moment, he moves closer to me. And I'm not certain how this is happening or why, but all of a sudden I am kissing Wyn Salvador.

And while I know that none of this is real, the smell of the tropics and the sound of the ocean and the feel of the breeze and his lips—so soft, how are they so soft?—convince my brain that it is very, *very* real.

And this is wrong, and we are in serious danger, and we should be trying right now to find another way to escape but for a moment I can't think, *I don't want to think*, and although I wanted to pulverize Wyn Salvador almost forty-eight hours ago, kissing him right now is very, *very* surprisingly good.

And as long as I am doing it, I don't have to think at all.

When I wake up hours later, we're still holding hands, though Wyn's grip has loosened somewhat, his face soft and shadowy in the moonlight. I study him, poring over the contours and details now that he's sleeping: the strong dark shape of his eyebrows, the soft curls of hair along his forehead, the long lashes that would be the envy of any cover girl, the slight dimples in his cheeks, the square of his jaw. The only flaw on his face, the only thing keeping it from perfection, is the way his mouth turns down at the corners again. Even in sleep Wyn is troubled, searching for answers.

Like I am.

I leave my hand in his and stare up at the night sky. I know the answer is inside me somewhere, I just need to find it. If I dreamed while I was asleep, I don't recall, but I do feel more clear-headed now, more focused. The bubbles did their work.

I go over the chain of events again, one by one:

1. Diego Salvador says that Wyn has barricaded himself inside the MEEP and left behind a suicide note.
2. The barricade is a type of maze, which several people before me fail to get through.
3. Once I conquer the maze, I enter Wyn's Havana via a portal in the Floridita.
4. I find Wyn (or he finds me), and he claims that he is trapped in the MEEP.
5. He denies both creating the maze and leaving behind the suicide note.
6. The portal in the Floridita disappears. Wyn's original portal is also gone.
7. Wyn claims there are human players in the MEEP with us. We capture one of them, who turns out to be Kora Lee, Diego Salvador's personal assistant.
8. Kora claims to be working for the Legionnaires, an anonymous group determined to shut down the MEEP.
9. Kora also claims they will kill her if she is captured.
10. Kora disappears, possibly dead.
11. Wyn Salvador and I truly and very thoroughly make out before falling asleep.

The last two puzzle pieces make me feel a little ill.

We—*I*—may have accidentally caused someone's death, so I used the opportunity to hook up with a guy I hardly know?

Seriously? What is wrong with me?

I try to remember what Wyn has said to me over and over: that it's not my fault, that I was just trying to save him, save myself, and Kora could have been bluffing. She was our last chance of finding a way out of here. We couldn't afford to let her go. And even if someone did hurt her—*kill* her even—it wasn't me.

But who was it? Who was she truly working for? The Legionnaires? Chang and Moose talk about LEGION all the time. As far as I know, it's just a bunch of kids like Chang who spend way too much time playing online games, sharing data, and grumbling about Diego Salvador's monopoly on MEEP technology. Sure, they might consider Salvador an enemy, but they wouldn't have the means to actually kidnap Wyn and blackmail his father. It makes much more sense to assume that Kora was working for some big tech firm or even a foreign government trying to get their hands on MEEP secrets—the kind of people who have the power and money to buy Kora's cooperation.

My next thought sends a chill down my spine. If those same people killed off Kora for blowing the operation, what's to keep them from doing the same to me if I get in their way? They don't need me; they need Wyn, and they need him to stay inside the MEEP.

Had Kora been on the Salvador estate when she was killed? I grimace at the thought.

I picture my body back in Wyn's room. I've been gone almost forty-eight hours and I must look the same as the Wyn I saw two days ago—my body attached to monitors and IV fluids, completely vulnerable to anyone who might wish me harm.

I shiver. Then I remember Dad sitting by my side, keeping vigil with Mama Beti. Those two will keep us safe. Heck, my dad would take on dragons before he'd let anyone harm me, and I'm pretty sure that on behalf of her beloved grandson, Mama Beti could do some damage with that metal walker of hers.

The thought almost makes me smile.

Beside me Wyn stirs and murmurs something in his sleep. After a moment he begins to rustle, as if agitated, though his eyes remain closed. He continues to speak, but the words are slurred and I can't make out what he's saying. He's having a nightmare, I can tell, and I can't decide whether I should leave him be or wake him up. When he cries out, as if in fright, I can stand it no longer.

"Wyn, wake up," I say, gently shaking him by the shoulder. "Wake up, you're having a bad dream."

His eyes open slowly, and I can still see fear there. As he stares at me, the fear begins to dissipate and relief washes over him. "Nixy," he whispers.

I reach over and lay a hand on his cheek, just like my mom

used to do when I had bad dreams. "It's over now," I say.

"I dreamed we were being buried alive," he says, sitting up in the recliner. "We were trapped in a deep pit and there were people above us—shadows, really—shoveling dirt on top of us. It was awful."

"That does sound awful," I agree, and my body shudders a bit. I don't say aloud what I'm thinking: Wyn's subconscious has painted a pretty accurate picture of our predicament. Gruesome, but accurate.

"All I could hear was Kora's voice saying *black* every time a new shovelful of dirt fell," says Wyn.

"That *was* a pretty dramatic last word," I say, remembering Kora's frightened face before she disappeared.

Wyn looks out at the city lights, his brow knitted in concentration. He gasps suddenly. "Nixy, what was the last thing you said to Kora, before she said *black*?" he asks, grabbing my arm, his voice now urgent.

I close my eyes and try to remember. "The portal," I say. "I asked her where they'd hid the portal."

It hits us both at the same time. Maybe Kora wasn't describing death with her last word. Maybe she was giving us a clue.

Wyn hops off the recliner, pulling me up with him.

"Come on," he says. "Over the river and through the woods. We're going to Grandma's house."

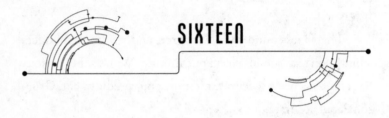

SIXTEEN

WYN TAKES THE STAIRS TO MAMA BETI'S BEDROOM BY TWOS AND I am right on his heels. We hardly spoke to each other on the motorcycle ride over here, but as we move to enter the room I pull on his arm to slow him down.

"Wait a minute, Wyn, we need to talk about this first. Tell me what you're planning to do."

"The Black, Nixy. You heard Kora. Maybe we can somehow get home through the Black."

"It's the *somehow* part that concerns me," I say, warily eyeing the door to the once-room, the now-nothing.

Wyn shrugs nonchalantly, though I wonder how much confidence he's pretending. "We'll just have to experiment. Tell me what you know about the Black."

"Very little," I admit. "Mostly that you probably shouldn't, you know, *experiment* with it." I feel a twinge of guilt as soon as I say this. I'd made a habit of tuning Chang out over the past year whenever he started telling horror stories about the Black. *It's just a game, Chang,* I'd say. *Those LEGION gearheads are just trying to scare you.* Now I wish I'd paid better attention to him, for more reasons than one. "For all I know, the Black is the Loch Ness Monster, with Frankenstein's head, on a giant spider body. It's all rumor and hearsay. *Dangerous* rumor and hearsay. But your father invented the MEEP. Surely you must know more about it than I do."

Wyn rubs his cheek. "All I've ever heard the programmers say about the Black is to leave it alone. Something to do with MEEP coding, and that the Black is actually part of your unconscious mind so the codes don't work there."

I peer again at the door into Mama Beti's room. A wave of shame washes over me as I think of all the beautiful work Wyn did on the other side—work that I ruined, leaving Godzilla-like destruction in my wake.

I turn back to him. "That's what my friend Chang says— that frequency codes can't reach you in the Black, and that some gamers have actually fried their short-term memories just by touching it."

Wyn looks skeptical. "That's impossible. Regular gamers wouldn't even have access to the Black. The MEEP protocols, even for custom-built worlds, provide for 360-degree safety walls. The only people who would ever encounter the Black are my dad's programmers."

"And us," I say, pointing to the door.

Wyn shrugs. "I'm not sure what happened here. I've never seen the Black in any of my custom worlds before. Maybe it's because I've used so many beta modules here? In any case, the story you heard can't be true. Regular players wouldn't have access to the Black."

"What about unauthorized players?"

Wyn frowns at me. "You mean hackers? Like LEGION? I don't know, Nixy, and I don't care. They take their own risks when they break into someone else's property."

"You sound like your father," I say, but without much bite behind it. I can't summon the nastiness. Not when we're both still reeling from our encounter with Kora and, well, whatever you call last night.

"Yeah, well, my dad has taken plenty of his own risks and it's about time for me to take one too," Wyn says. "Maybe the Black will reset us back to the Landing . . . or even better, wake us up back at home."

He pulls away from me and throws the door open. The Black is just on the other side.

It is a gaping, jagged oval taking up the entire door frame. The insides are kinetic, shimmery and spongy . . . like a brain, I guess. Alive, somehow. As before, a shudder of revulsion comes over me when I look into it, a shadow of fear. I can tell Wyn feels it too by the grimace on his face.

"Are you sure we should be messing with this?" I ask.

"Absolutely not, but what choice do we have? Someone may have killed Kora in the real world. What's to keep them from killing us next?"

"You," I say. "*You're* what's keeping them from killing us next. As long as you're alive, they have power over your father, Wyn. If you die, they have nothing." I pause and shrug. "Me? I suppose I'm pretty expendable at this point. Probably even a liability in their eyes."

That last point does not sit well with Wyn. "All the more reason to get out of here this very minute. Come on. What have we got to lose?"

"Our minds?" I offer, glancing at the Black.

Wyn ignores this. "We'll go together on the count of three," he says, taking my hand.

"No way," I argue, pulling him away from the hole. "I'll go by myself. If it *does* work and I get out of here, I'll come right back for you, I promise. If it nukes my noggin instead, well, at least one of us will still have a working brain to figure out Plan B." Wyn doesn't think this is funny. "I should be the one to take the risk," I insist.

He holds my gaze. "I don't want . . . you shouldn't have to do this. Not for me."

I know he's trying to say more than the words coming out of his mouth.

I shake my head and try to pull off the same magic trick, to say the things I want to say, but don't have time for.

"There are only a few people I *would* do it for—and since you're the one I happened to be trapped here with—"

"But, I—"

"Think, Wyn," I say, cutting him off. "What if I do get kicked back to the Landing? I know exactly how to get through the maze now, exactly how to defeat the enemies. I can be back in a flash. You? It will take you forever to fight your way through, and I don't have that kind of time."

Wyn finally rewards me with a small smile. "Hey now, pretty full of yourself, aren't you, Nixy Bauer?"

"Only when I know I'm right."

Wyn rubs his lips together, then nods. "Okay, I concede. But go slowly, and if anything feels wrong then come right back out."

"Roger that," I say, swallowing the last bit of fear that's been camped in my throat. No reason to be a scaredy-pants at this stage of the game. Not after everything I've been through.

Wyn is still holding my left hand, so I mentally brace myself and stick my right hand into the Black. I expect it to feel gelatinous inside, but instead I feel nothing, like I've just put my hand through a cloud. I wave my arm around for a second, feeling, reaching for I-don't-know-what. A button would be nice, a big fat GAME OVER button, but I know that's wishful thinking.

"All right, I'm going in," I say. "You wait for me right here in Mama Beti's house, okay?"

Wyn nods. "Good luck," he says, but he doesn't let go of my hand even when I try to tug it away.

"You're going to have to let go of me at some point," I say, smiling.

"I know," he says, returning the smile, "but not until the very last second."

This time it's my turn to give him a good-bye wink, which I hope comes off as jaunty, and I step inside the Black.

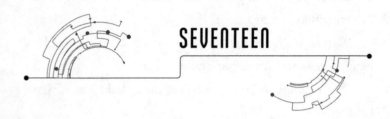

SEVENTEEN

THE WORLD GOES PITCH DARK. I CANNOT MOVE.

Terror seizes my heart.

The Black is all around me.

A single thought pulses through my brain.

Don't breathe it in, can't breathe it in, don't let it get inside me.

I feel it, like a dense fog pressing up against my face.

I hold my breath, but it is no use.

I can feel it invading my body, creeping in through my nostrils, seeping through my pores.

I try to call out but my face is stone, unable to make a sound.

Dread.

The feeling floods my brain.

I can't move.

I am stone.

Every muscle, petrified.

And now the pain begins.

It starts in my lower body, like someone is holding a match to each one of my toes. I want to thrash, move away from the fire, but I'm paralyzed.

The burning licks up my legs.

I scream and cry. I beg for help.

No sound comes out of my mouth.

The fire is in my torso now. The heat is melting my organs, incinerating my bones.

The pain consumes me.

NO! Make it stop. Make it stop. Make it stop!

I am burning alive.

Another moment and the heat will reach my brain.

And I will be dead.

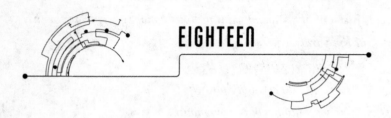

EIGHTEEN

"NIXY!"

I am stone, I am dead.

"Nixy, wake up! Please, look at me!"

I feel a hand on my face, stroking my cheek.

"Please . . ."

I see color through my eyelids. The darkness is gone. I try to open my eyes, but the lids are so heavy, leaden, I can only lift them a sliver.

"That's it! Come back, come back to me."

The hand is running through my hair now. I remember someone doing this to me when I was younger, when I was alive. Someone who loved me.

Mom?

I come back to myself in a rush, a tidal wave. I remember who I am now. I am Nixy Bauer and something bad happened, but Jill is here now. Everything will be okay.

I slowly force my eyes open.

"Thank God," says a voice above me. It is not my mother's.

A salty sea breeze drifts across my face and I breathe it in. The person behind the voice slowly comes into focus. Brown curly hair, brown eyes, long lashes.

"Nixy, are you okay?" He is kneeling on the floor beside me, one hand still on my face, the other hand resting awkwardly in his lap.

I struggle to remember his name.

Wyn?

Wyn Salvador.

I gasp. I remember now. I'm in the MEEP. *Trapped* in the MEEP.

"Where's Kora?" I ask him. "Did she get away? We need to go after her."

Wyn blinks. He seems confused.

I look around and see we're in Mama Beti's house, the hall-way lights twinkling above me. "What are we doing here?" I ask, wondering *why* exactly I'm lying on the floor.

"You don't . . . you don't remember," Wyn says. It is not a question.

I search my memory, trying to recall the circumstances in

which we came to be in this unusual position. The last thing I remember is uncovering Kora at the Tropicana but I don't remember where she went after that, what we did with her. I shake my head. "Sorry, I—what'd I miss?"

Wyn smiles. It's a strange, rueful grin. Then he glances down at his right hand, which, now that I get a good look at it, appears to have had several bones removed.

"Did Kora do that to you?" I ask, propping myself up on my elbows. This sudden surge of anger makes me feel like my old self again. "Because I will take her down."

Wyn shakes his head. "No, it wasn't Kora."

"Then how? Who?"

"You," he says, almost apologetically.

My mouth drops open and I pull myself up to sitting. "No."

"Yes," Wyn says, getting to his feet. He offers me his good hand and hauls me off the floor.

I stand, unsteadily at first. Wyn circles an arm around my waist and I swivel away. Whoa. What is that about? "Hey, hands to yourself, buddy," I half joke.

Wyn stares for a moment. "Just to be clear, you don't remember *anything* after spotting Kora. Like, *nothing*. Nothing at all."

For some reason, I'm embarrassed. "No. Was there something... important?"

He sighs. "I'll tell you about it on the way there."

"The way *where*?"

"You'll see," says Wyn, leading me through the rubble and out of the room. "But first we've got a date with Larry."

Larry. I smile. At least, thankfully, I remember him.

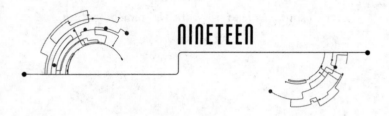

NINETEEN

"BRRRAAAAAOOOKKKK!"

Larry, it seems, is excited to see us. As the kraken speeds toward us on the seawall I try to look cool and collected, but it's hard not to break out my crossbow and start pumping arrows into him. He's a kraken, after all, and a mighty big one.

Wyn must see the flash of panic cross my face because he puts his good hand on my shoulder.

I'm not sure why he has a sudden onset of the touchy-feelies, but I handle it a little more gracefully this time.

"Remember, none of this is real," Wyn says, just as Larry raises a beastly tentacle and splashes us.

The cold water makes me gasp. "Well, it *feels* real," I say, somewhat less enamored of Wyn's world and its cutting-edge sensory modules than I once was.

On the walk here, Wyn filled me in on my memory lapse. Kora is dead. Or at least, we think she is. And then, apparently, like an idiot, I willingly stepped into the Black. Wyn doesn't know what happened to me there, but I guess I started screaming bloody murder. He said it sounded like someone was torturing me, like I had gone stark raving mad with pain and fear.

Fortunately, he was still holding my hand at that point and somehow managed to pull me back to the MEEP.

*Un*fortunately, I squeezed his hand so tightly I did some major damage to his avatar.

I glance down again at his limp hand.

"I told you, it doesn't hurt," he assures me. "It's just useless until I gulp down a healing potion."

"Right. So what are we doing here?" I ask, jumping as Larry extends one of his purple tentacles in my direction.

"Going for a ride," Wyn replies just as Larry wraps a tentacle around us and lifts us in the air.

"What the hell? What the hell?!" I yell as Larry starts thrashing through the sea. He has the two of us raised in the air over his head, like a five-year-old holding an ice cream cone. Wyn and I are squished into each other. Full-frontal togetherness, with our arms pinned to our sides.

Awkward doesn't even begin to describe how this feels to

me. Wyn, on the other hand, seems weirdly at ease. Comfortable enough to crack jokes.

"So how do you like the view?" he asks, trying to keep a straight face.

I can't help it. I burst out laughing. "Do you mean the one of the ocean or the two tiny freckles near your ear? Because if you're talking about the freckles, I think they're a divine enhancement. Let me guess: you used a buy-one-get-one-free coupon at the Freckles Emporium?"

Wyn makes a face. "I'll have you know my avatar is one hundred percent me, right down to the very last freckle."

Larry does a little twirl in the water now, like a ballerina, and I look over my shoulder to see where we're headed.

"See that little isle in the distance?" Wyn says, pointing with his chin.

I nod. A small dome of land rises in the middle of the crystal-blue water, its sandy white beach topped by lush green palm trees.

"That's where we're going. It's where I keep all the good stuff stashed."

A few minutes later Larry is reluctantly setting us ashore. Wyn picks up a fallen coconut from the beach and waves it at the kraken. Larry's bulbous eyeballs grow even bigger as he swims back out a few yards, his tentacles waving in anticipation. Wyn heaves the coconut, which Larry catches expertly.

"My turn," I say, and pitch two more.

Larry juggles the three coconuts like a circus clown while Wyn and I whistle and hoot in appreciation. Finally, Larry pops the coconuts in his beak, waves good-bye, and sinks back under the sea.

Wyn motions for me to follow him. We head up the beach until we get to a break in the palm trees, then take a path carved through the vegetation. After a minute we reach a clearing and I bark out a laugh.

"You built a treehouse?" I say, shaking my head at the elaborate construction in front of me. It looks like something straight out of *Swiss Family Robinson* or *Gilligan's Island*, every kid's childhood fantasy.

Wyn looks half embarrassed, half proud. "It was my first custom creation in the MEEP. I've always wanted a treehouse, ever since I was little, so I decided to make one for myself."

"Well done," I say, admiring the multilevel open-air architecture. "Rustic, yet charming at the same time."

"Wait until you see the waterfall shower in the back. Come on, I'll show you around."

We go up and down a dozen ladders, slides, and rope bridges—slowly, since Wyn has to do everything one-handed—and peek into a dozen different rooms. We finally end up on a platform high above the tree line.

"This is where I like to sleep," Wyn says, pointing to a big woven hammock strung between bamboo poles.

"Under the stars—I should have known," I say, admiring the view from this bird's-eye perch. The entire island is surrounded by a ring of brilliant white sand and sparkling blue water beyond that. In the distance I see a pod of dolphins cavorting.

Wyn opens a cabinet and pulls out a first-aid kit. The kit contains a dozen small bottles lined up in a row like colorful soldiers. He selects a green potion and holds it to the light. "This should do it," he says, and glugs it down. Then he holds his mangled hand out in front of him and together we watch it shimmer and waver. Then, *pop*, it takes proper shape again. "Just like new."

"You don't happen to have any 'beam me up, Scotty' potions or ruby slippers in that cabinet, do you?" I ask, only half joking.

Wyn shakes his head. "Sorry. I never even used to keep healing potions here, but once I started playing with Larry, I figured it was a good idea. Especially after the one time he hugged me a little too hard."

I nod, remembering the anaconda that nearly squeezed me down a few dress sizes. "I suppose a hug from Larry could crack a rib or two."

"Exactly. After that I decided to keep some potions on hand in case it happened again."

"And what's this?" I ask, picking up what looks like a remote control sitting on top of the cabinet.

"Ah," says Wyn, taking it from me. "You're going to love this." He clicks a button. Instantly, a tarp rolls out above our heads just as a rumble of thunder shakes the treehouse and rain begins to fall.

It's a slow, steady rain, the kind that feels soothing, cleansing almost, as it falls around you. "You're right, I do love it," I say, sticking a hand out to feel the drops. "Show me more."

Wyn hands the remote back to me and I experiment with all the buttons. I make it rain harder, then softer, then I roll up the tarp and let the sun back out. I change day to dusk, dusk to night, and night back to day again. I scrutinize the MEEP MAIL icon. "I don't suppose . . ."

Wyn gives me an impatient look. "Believe me, it was one of the first things I tried. They must have cut off all communication frequencies. Can't receive mail, can't send it."

"Right," I say, trying to ignore his tone. Of course Wyn's already tried everything. Still, I had to ask, didn't I? Because maybe there's one small thing he missed. One little crack in the armor surrounding us.

"Try the banana icon," Wyn suggests, a hint of apology in his voice.

I press a button on the remote and a family of monkeys appears in the trees around us, chittering among themselves in friendly fashion. I smile as a baby monkey takes a seat on Wyn's shoulder, and Wyn grins back at me. I turn up the temperature to "tropical," and even though we can't sweat in the MEEP—thank God—somehow I still register, still *feel*, the extra intensity of the sun.

"Whew! Easy there, before our avatars melt," Wyn says, reaching up to give the baby monkey a scratch between the ears. "How about a swim to cool off?"

I look down at the gorgeous beach. I'd love nothing more than to splash through those waves right now, but we've got work to do. "Shouldn't we go back? Or at least come up with a new plan?"

"Go back where, Nixy? And do what? Our last plan nearly killed you."

"Oh, don't be so dramatic. Yes, I lost my memory for a bit but it was hardly a life-or-death situation."

"That's because you don't remember it, Nixy, but I do. I had to listen to you scream. You were in so much pain you *crushed* my hand. If I had let go . . ."

"Fine," I concede. "But you're just proving my point. We need to figure out our next move. Not take a vacation."

"What move? I've been trying to bust out of here for days. There's *nothing* we can do. Going back to Havana's not going to help, not right now anyway. Here on the island we have total privacy. There aren't any Meeple or portals, so there's no way for anyone to spy on us. Remember, Rico Suave's still out there somewhere."

"And when I find him I'm going to rip his arms out. Maybe

even mess up his perfect hair," I joke. As I'd hoped, the serious look on Wyn's face turns to a smile again. I like him better this way, I realize.

And all of a sudden, I feel tired of worrying, tired of anger, tired of thinking. I find myself wondering, *Why not take a little break?* My brain deals better with knotty problems when they're on the back burner, anyway.

And, of course, there is the part I don't tell Wyn.

I have the distinct feeling there is something else I have forgotten. Something Wyn hasn't told me.

"Wyn—" I begin, but then I lose my nerve.

"What is it? Tell me," he says, the smile still playing on his lips.

"You did tell me everything, right? Everything that happened after we trapped Kora?"

Wyn's face goes slack and his eyes skitter away from mine.

"Everything important," he finally says, turning back to me. "Are you sure you don't remember anything at all?" His eyes are searching mine now, as if he's trying to find the memories inside of me.

But there are none.

I shake my head.

Wyn's shoulders slump and he looks away again.

"Never mind," I say, feeling more confused than ever. "Let's go swim."

The water feels delicious—not too cold, not too warm, but

that just-right temperature that almost never happens in the real world. I let the waves tumble me around in the shallows like a piece of driftwood while Wyn bodysurfs nearby. He's changed into bright green swim trunks and I'm wearing the most suitable thing I could find in my virtual closet—the tiny little dress I wore to level Coop. That seems like years ago now instead of weeks. In any case, the dress is small enough to look like a one-piece skirted swimsuit, and it's better than swimming in cargo pants or drowning in the wench dress.

I try my best to enjoy this picture-perfect moment and give my brain a rest, but it's harder than it should be. Images of Kora, Rico Suave, Diego Salvador, and even the damn sharks from the maze keep appearing before my eyes. I try to push the images away, back to the no-man's-land part of my brain, to save for later. I don't want to think about them now.

I remember the meditation exercises Jill makes me do whenever I'm stressing about school and college too much. I close my eyes for a moment and try to empty my mind. I focus on the sound of the waves around me, the smell of salt in the air. I hold my breath and duck under the water. The images in my head slowly disappear and everything goes dark.

The water presses in around me.

Black.

I stifle a scream.

Memory of the Black overwhelms every thought, every sense I have.

Pain.

Fire.

Death.

No, not again!

I snap my eyes back open and pull myself up from the water.

I break the surface and search for Wyn.

I don't see him. I call his name and start to panic. I pump my arms and legs, thrashing in a full circle, searching the water for him.

"Wyn!" I scream, just as he surfaces down the shore from me, shaking the water from his body like a dog. He turns and waves, a big grin on his face.

Wyn.

I calm myself and wave back.

Just stay with Wyn, I tell myself.

Wyn will keep me safe.

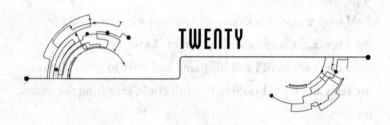

TWENTY

"HOW LONG HAVE WE BEEN HERE?" I SAY AS WE FOLLOW A PATH through the island jungle. I am picking ripe berries from the foliage and tossing them to our monkey friends in the treetops. They squeal with pleasure as they take flying leaps from tree to tree.

"Three days," Wyn says, glancing at me in concern.

He's worried about me, I can tell.

And honestly, *I'm* worried about me.

We don't talk about it but we both know.

I've changed.

I'm not me anymore.

I'm scared.

Scared of feeling pain again, the excruciating pain of the Black.

Scared to do anything at all that might make it return.

Scared to leave the island.

I even refuse to go into the sea now, afraid of its murky depths, afraid of losing myself in its darkness.

So we go for walks instead. We play catch with Larry and pick fruit with the monkeys. We catch our own fish from the island streams, grill it on the beach, and wash it down with guava juice. We don't remind each other that it's only virtual food and drink, that our real bodies are back home being pumped full of IV fluids to keep us alive. We don't remind ourselves that we're running out of time. We don't talk about our latest strategy, because we don't have one.

The fact is, the only plan I can think of is to go back to Havana, hope that Rico Suave shows up again, and pray that we can successfully ambush him this time. Oh, and then convince him to tell us more than Kora did. It is a lot to hope for. *Too much* to hope for. And besides, I don't want to go back to Havana. The Black is there.

"Tell me more about your childhood," I say, trying to take my mind off our troubles. I like hearing Wyn talk about his life before his mom died, how she used to take him with her on her musical tours, about the adventures they had together in Paris and Rome and Buenos Aires. It all sounds so perfect, like a fairy tale.

"What more would you like to know?" asks Wyn, popping

a berry into his mouth. "Pretty sure I've told you all the good parts by now."

"Did your mom sing you to sleep when you were little?" I ask. "My dad used to sing me Irish drinking songs every night. I'd usually fall asleep after a few rounds of 'Nancy Whiskey' and a 'Danny Boy' or two." I belt out a few lines of "Nancy Whiskey" in my best Irish brogue and Wyn rewards me with a grin.

"Can't say my mom ever lulled me to sleep with pub songs," he answers, "but she did read me nursery rhymes every night. She had a big illustrated *Mother Goose* book that she'd kept from her own childhood."

"You mean like 'Mary Had a Little Lamb' and 'Itsy Bitsy Spider'? You must have fallen asleep instantly," I tease.

Wyn gives me a little push and I return a light elbow. "It wasn't *that* boring," he says. "Sometimes we'd have a contest and change the words, to see who could make the other laugh."

"Give me an example," I say. We've reached the homemade jungle swings Wyn made yesterday while I waded in the nearby stream with my fishing net.

"Well, pick a nursery rhyme and I'll make one up for you," Wyn says as we start swinging.

"'Little Miss Muffet,'" I order as I pump my legs beside him.

He quickly obliges. "Little Miss Bauer sat in her tower, eating a burger and fries. Along came a spider who sat down beside her and said, 'I prefer zee french flies.'"

I shove his swing with my foot. "That's so bad it's almost good. *Almost.*"

"And I suppose you spent your childhood engaged in much more sophisticated activities like studying Latin and practicing your posture?" he asks, shoving me back.

"Not even a little bit," I answer, remembering ragtag summers spent running around the neighborhood with Chang and Moose. The memories make me smile.

"Then what *did* you do?" Wyn asks.

"I've told you about Chang and Moose, right? When we were really little, preschool even, Chang used to orchestrate these absurd games for the three of us to play. No matter how crazy they were, Moose and I would always go along with them, just to see what Chang would do next."

"What kind of absurd games?" Wyn asks.

I think back thirteen years ago. "Well, so one rainy afternoon Chang makes an elaborate fort out of couch cushions and tells us it's a drive-through restaurant called Nacho Burger," I begin. While I talk I start pushing myself in circles, twisting the ropes of my swing into a tight spiral. Wyn does the same with his. "So Moose and I pretend to drive through in our imaginary cars and we place our orders. Moose orders nachos. 'We don't have any nachos,' Chang hollers at him. So then I come through and order a burger. 'We don't have any burgers,' Chang hollers at me. 'So what *do* you have?' Moose and I both ask, baffled. 'Chicken!' he yells, like we're total idiots, then slams the couch cushion window shut in a fury. Moose and I laughed the rest of the day . . . we still laugh about it sometimes. And for years we used to beg Chang to play Nacho Burger again."

"So, how many Nacho Burger adventures did you have?" Wyn asks. Our swings are now wound all the way up to the top.

I shake my head. "Just the one. Chang was always on to something new, quickly bored by us lesser mortals. He's too smart for his own good, if you know what I mean. Always two steps ahead of everyone else." I look up at our tightly wound swings. "Me, I'm much more easily amused."

Wyn grins at me. "Ready?"

"Ready," I say, and we both release our swings.

Wyn bellows and I shriek as the vines spin us around like wind-up toys. We're going so fast that by the time we unspin all the way, our swings dump us into a heap on the ground.

We stumble to our feet and stagger around like dizzy, punch-drunk sailors. I grab Wyn's arm for support and pull him off balance instead. We topple back down to the ground, laughing, but now Wyn is on top of me, and we find ourselves pinned to each other again, face-to-face. Our laughs die into smiles and neither one of us moves.

Wyn's face softens as he looks into my eyes.

"Wyn—" I start to say, because I know what's coming next. "I'm not sure we should—"

"Don't worry," he whispers, tenderly brushing the hair away from my face. "None of this is real, remember?"

And then he rises from the ground, pulling me to my feet.

There is something sad in his face.

Again, it's something I'm missing. I know it. Something I have forgotten.

More than before, I have the sense that it is something worth fighting for. Something that I want to get back. Something that matters in the real world, not just here in the MEEP.

I look across the water toward Havana.

It sits darkened in a shadow thrown by a passing cloud.

Wyn beckons me toward the treehouse. "Snack, rock star?"

And in that moment, the real world seems farther away than ever.

For a moment, I wonder if I can ever return. If I *should* ever return.

I walk away from the swings.

And walk away from that thought for another day.

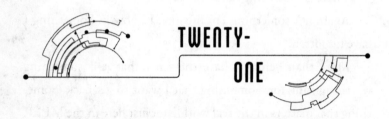

TWENTY-ONE

I AM SLEEPING SO SWEETLY. SO DEEPLY, SO DREAMLESSLY. I DO NOT want to wake up. I want to stay here forever, but someone is knocking on the door.

Go away, I think. *I'm not here.*

I pull the blanket over my head.

The knocking continues. It is a soft knock, but insistent.

I try to ignore it, nestling inside my flannel cocoon. My blanket smells a little bit like fabric softener, a little bit like Hodee. It smells like home.

Home!

My eyes fly open.

I'm in my room. My room!

It's dark in here, but on the wall opposite me I see the

Pikachu nightlight that Chang and Moose gave me for my seventh birthday. My heart swells.

I am home, I am home, I am home.

The knocking starts again.

"Mom?" I call, sitting up in bed. "Dad?"

I am wearing my usual pajamas, a worn pair of yoga pants and an old Cubs T-shirt. I have never been so happy to see these clothes. I have never been so happy to see my parents.

But why don't they come in? There's no lock on my bedroom door.

I leap from my bed, cross the room, and fling the door open.

The hallway is empty.

And dark.

"Mom?" I yell, sweeping my hand along the wall for the light switch.

I flip it on.

Nothing.

I try again, flipping the switch up and down several times.

Still nothing.

"Dad?" I yell, running back to my nightstand to turn on the bedside lamp.

Click click click.

Nothing.

I rest my hand over my pounding heart, willing it to slow

down. I'm home. No need to panic. The power went out. That is all.

Bam!

The bedroom door slams shut behind me.

My heart is racing now, my breath coming out in ragged gasps.

"Mom! Dad!" I yell again, searching the nightstand, floor, bed, for my phone and its flashlight app. I can't find it anywhere.

I stare at the door. Who closed it? Hodee! Maybe Hodee nudged it shut. Maybe, *maybe*, I think—my mind searching wildly for an answer, for some reasonable explanation—maybe he was so excited by my return that he ran into the door and pushed it shut by mistake.

I yell Hodee's name and reach for the doorknob, but a competing voice in my head warns me to stop, tells me that I'm wrong, that this is absurd, that there *is* no reasonable explanation. I push it away and open the door.

"Hodee! Mom! Dad!" I call, stumbling through the dark hallway. "Where are you?"

Behind me my bedroom door slams shut again.

This time I scream.

I run to the end of the hallway to my parents' room. I turn the knob, but the door is locked. I pound on the door, yelling for my parents. I try the knob again.

The hallway grows darker.

I am crying now, sobbing.

I run through the hall trying every door.

The bathroom door.

Locked.

My mom's office.

Locked.

I hear a door slam downstairs.

A shudder rushes through me, raising every last hair on my body.

Who is in the house with me?

Why won't they answer?

I stand at the top of the stairwell, the sound of my own heart exploding inside my head. I clasp a hand over my mouth, trying to stifle the sobs. I need to be still, I need to listen. Who is down there?

I will my body to cooperate. I take deep breaths to slow my breathing. I wrap my arms around my rib cage to stop the shivering. I bite my lip to keep from screaming.

I listen.

There is only silence.

Maybe they've left.

Have they left?

And then I hear it.

A faint whisper.

"Nixy!"

The sound comes from behind me.

My stomach clenches in fear.

"Momma?" I murmur, slowly turning around.

There is no one there. Just a long, dark hallway.

I hear it again.

"Nixy!"

The voice is so quiet I can barely hear it, yet urgent and familiar at the same time. And it is coming from my bedroom. The door now stands ajar. Pikachu's dim light casts an eerie glow inside.

I slowly walk toward the room, then pause in the doorway.

"Nixy!"

The voice is coming from under the bed.

I taste blood and realize I have bitten through my lip.

"Momma?" I whimper, sinking to my knees.

Don't look, don't look, don't look, my mind shrieks.

But I have to look.

I have to.

Haltingly, I lower myself to all fours, then bend my elbows. I lean my head down, eyes squeezed shut.

I start to open them when I feel someone's breath on my neck.

"Nixy!"

I open my mouth and scream instead.

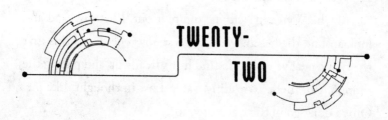

TWENTY-TWO

I BOLT UPRIGHT.

I'm on the beach. A full moon casts its sparkling light over the sea. The waves roll in gently, thrumming their way across the sand.

I'm still in the MEEP.

Thank God. I was only dreaming.

I lie back down and cover my face with my hands, still shaken by the nightmare.

I want so badly to be home. But not *that* home.

I know the dream is my subconscious trying to tell me something, but what? The darkness, the locked rooms . . . surely they're some kind of metaphor for the Black and my lost memories . . . but holy hell, does my brain really need to torment me like this? Haven't I been through enough already without my own brain cells turning against me?

That creepy voice whispering to me, stalking me. Who was it? I feel like I should know.

Maybe Wyn can help me figure it out. I lift my head and look around the beach. We often rest down here, and this isn't the first time I've woken to find him already up and pacing the shore. Or in the sea, treading water. Lost in thought, like me. Only I don't go in the water anymore.

I finally spot him, emerging from the waves several yards away. In the corner of my eye, I also spy a flicker, a shadow, in the treeline. A human-shaped shadow.

I'm not the only one watching Wyn.

I freeze, then carefully lower my head back down to the sand, my eyes glued to the shadow.

Wyn stops to shake the water off himself, then walks up the beach toward the tree line. The shadow crouches below the brush, hiding from Wyn.

Someone has breeched our island.

Someone who does not wish to be seen.

I quickly weigh my options. If I call out to Wyn, the stalker will no doubt run away or disappear. That just leaves one other choice.

I have to stalk the stalker.

I wait until Wyn disappears into the forest and the shadow

after him, before I dare move. Then I scramble up the beach, keeping my head low.

"Inventory!" I whisper into the MEEPosphere, then select my night-vision goggles and a laser gun.

I pause at the trailhead where they disappeared, which leads back to the treehouse. Good. I know this path well, which gives me an advantage over the stalker. I tuck myself behind a tree and peer through my goggles. Wyn walks the middle of the trail, clearly visible in the moonlight. The stalker remains several paces behind him, keeping in the shadows of the trees. Though I can't see his face, I can tell by his shape that he is tall and large and male.

I continue several paces behind, laser gun ready, waiting for my shot. If I can just manage to shoot the stalker in the leg, wound him enough to slow him down but not kill him, I might be able to catch him.

As we near the treehouse, a twig snaps under the stalker's foot. He dodges behind a tree as Wyn whips his head around.

"Nixy?" Wyn calls.

Damn.

I remain frozen behind my own tree.

For a moment, all I hear is the forest's usual nighttime hum.

Slowly, carefully, I peer out from my hiding place. Wyn has gone still, his eyes scanning the forest around him. Then he shrugs and continues to the treehouse.

As we arrive at the compound, I wait in the shadows, planning my next move. Wyn begins climbing the rope ladders to the rooftop platform. The stalker waits for him to ascend the first level, then follows him like a ninja.

Whoever he is, he's good.

I circle around the compound and quickly, quietly, scale the wooden planks of an adjacent tree. I cut across a rope bridge to a small perch among the highest treetops. From here I have a perfect view of the platform—I adjust my night-vision goggles—and a perfect shot.

I watch as Wyn's head finally appears through the platform's trapdoor. He picks up the remote, then reclines in the hammock.

Is he going to sleep?

I'm a little put out that he's left me alone on the beach—at least for all he knows—but I don't have time to get bent out of shape. A moment later the stalker's head pops through the opening.

Well, I'll be damned.

If it isn't Rico Suave.

Though I'd love to shoot the handsome right off his face, a laser gun to the head will surely kill him. Instead I bide my time and wait for him to finish climbing the ladder. When his full body finally emerges, I train my sights on his legs.

As I pull the trigger, Wyn shoots up from the hammock,

remote still in hand, and launches himself at Rico.

"No!" I yell, but it's too late to stop my gun. It fires straight at them as they fall to the floor, locked together like wrestlers.

"*Fy fæn*," I mutter, trying to make out the jumble of limbs on the platform. Which one did I shoot?

"Rappelling gun!" I shout, then use it to Tarzan my way over to them.

As I swing onto the platform, Rico Suave gets to his knees. Oh God.

That means . . .

Wyn lies on the floor, one hand pressed to his heart.

"Wyn!" I yell, but he's raising the remote at Rico. He doesn't see me.

"Attack," he cries, pressing a button, then slumps lifeless to the floor.

A huge screech vibrates from the trees. Rico and I both look up as a horde of monkeys starts skittering across the tree-tops toward us.

Rico doesn't waste any time. In an impressive feat of gymnastics he hurtles himself back down the ladders. I take one glance at Wyn, but I know there's nothing I can do for him right now. I have to catch Rico.

We race back down the main trail, only this time Rico's the prey instead of Wyn. The monkeys and I chase after him, thrashing through the trees and brush. Several times I raise my laser gun and pull the trigger, but Rico is too fast, too evasive, for me to land a shot.

Rico Suave's got skills.

When we emerge at the beach, the monkeys and I are still several paces behind him.

Rico picks up a last-minute burst of speed and heads for the water.

I can't let him get there.

I tear off my goggles, throw down my gun, and take a flying leap. I grab for him, wrapping both hands around his ankle.

We fall to the ground.

Only we hit water.

No.

The darkness swallows me.

Not this. Not this again.

Rico struggles inside my grip, thrashing his leg to release my hold.

Don't you dare let go, I order myself.

But I am seized with terror.

The darkness consumes me.

I can't do it.

I can't.

I let go of Rico's leg and scramble to the surface.

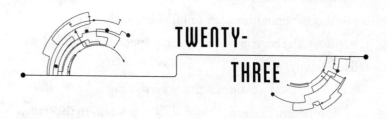

TWENTY-
THREE

"I CAN'T BELIEVE I *KILLED* YOU," I SAY AGAIN, RAKING MY FINGERS through my hair. "And then I let that *rasshøl* get away." I am furious with myself.

We are back at the treehouse, but Wyn has made it morning, the sun big and bright on the horizon. After Wyn regenerated and came back to life, he wasted no time securing our defenses. First he directed our monkey friends to form a lookout around the island. Then he ordered Larry to swim the perimeter and guard us with his hoary tentacles.

Since then, we'd been filling each other in on the evening's events.

"I keep telling you, it's not your fault," Wyn says from the hammock.

I shake my head. I don't argue with him anymore, but it *is* my fault. No doubt about it.

Wyn almost had the guy last night, before I screwed things up. He'd noticed Rico spying on him while he was swimming. So he'd come up with a plan to lure him to the treehouse and trap him with the help of our monkey friends. All while I was safely sleeping.

Only instead of sleeping, I was sabotaging his efforts. Unintentionally, of course, but still . . . I shot him in the *heart*.

Brilliant.

And after all that, I didn't even have the guts to hang on to Rico when I had him.

I pull on my hair. I haven't helped Wyn at all. I've only hurt him.

I am the worst leveller ever.

I glance up at the hammock and watch Wyn drift back to sleep. He still hasn't regained his full strength yet, and he is tired.

I'm tired too, but there's no way I'm going back to sleep. Last evening's nightmare is too fresh in my mind, that familiar, whispery voice summoning me.

Nixy!

I shiver, remembering the breath on my neck.

Who was it? Who was calling me?

I hear it again.

Nixy!

All of a sudden, I know.

I know who it is.

It's me. It's *my* voice.

And I know what I need to do.

I have to swallow my fear.

I have to look under the bed.

For real this time.

"Are you sure you want to do this?" Wyn says, taking my hand.

I nod slowly as his brown eyes lock onto mine. "I'm sure."

He squeezes my hand. "There's nothing to be afraid of, I promise."

I swallow and close my eyes. I'm *not* sure I'm ready for this, but I have to try.

"On three, then," Wyn says.

I nod again, but keep my eyes shut.

"One," he says, "two—"

Wyn doesn't wait for three. He yanks my hand and we go careening off the cliff together.

I scream all the way down, cycling my legs furiously until we hit the water below.

WHOOSH.

The impact of our fall drives us straight to the bottom of the bay.

The coral-blue water turns to dark.

It's nearly black down here.

I'd keep screaming, but I'm forced to hold my breath instead.

My feet touch the sandy bottom and I push hard, propelling myself back to the surface.

Wyn and I are still holding hands.

I spit water out of my mouth and blink as the radiant sun sparkles overhead.

Wyn whoops loudly. "You did it, Nixy, you did it!"

"I did it," I say softly, then raise my voice to the sky. "I did it!"

Damn the Black. I'm tired of being scared.

I will not be afraid of the dark any longer.

Now Wyn is twirling me around in the water. "Woo-hoo! Look out, world, Nixy Badass Bauer is back!"

I can't help myself. I start to laugh.

I may even be crying a little bit, I'm not sure.

I hear the familiar sound of my phone vibrating and I reach a sleepy hand over to turn it off. Only my phone feels different somehow, the buttons in the wrong place. I open my eyes.

Right, the MEEP. Sleep has discombobulated me once again.

After our jump, Wyn and I decided to take one last restorative nap before summoning Larry to take us back to Havana.

We don't have a plan yet, but we can't hide here on the island any longer. We need to go *do* something. *Anything*. And we need to have all our wits about us when we do.

Wyn hasn't been able to get out, but somehow he's survived here. And somehow I made it in. Which means his captors, our captors, have blind spots. We only have to find them to exploit them.

The remote vibrates in my hand again and I squint at it. The MEEP MAIL icon is flashing.

I blink. This can't be right.

I walk over to Wyn's hammock. "Hey," I say softly in his ear.

Wyn murmurs something unintelligible and rolls his head away from me.

"Hey," I repeat, a little more loudly this time, and gently shake his shoulder.

He opens his eyes and smiles at me. He looks so sweet I almost want to sink into the hammock next to him, but this may be important. "I thought you said you haven't been able to send or receive mail here."

"That's right," he says.

I hold the remote in front of him. "Look."

Wyn's eyes widen as they register the blinking icon and he takes the remote from me. He presses the button and reads. I'm dying to look over his shoulder to see what the message says but

I restrain myself. Instead I look down at my virtual fingernails and pick at them nervously.

"It's for you," Wyn says, his voice unreadable, and hands me the remote.

"What?" I say, thinking he must be teasing, but his face has turned dark, worried again.

I bite my lip and read the message.

NIXY, THERE'S A PORTAL THROUGH THE TOMB. GO ALONE.

I stiffen. "Who sent this?" I ask, scrutinizing the message as if somehow I can figure out who the sender is just by staring at it long enough. "What does this mean, Wyn?"

Wyn rubs his jaw. "I don't know. Maybe it means they're letting you go. Maybe they just want me."

"What if it's a trap?" I reply, thinking of Kora's demise. "If they were going to let me go, why would they wait this long?"

Wyn shakes his head. "Agreed. I don't like it. Not one bit."

"But if it is a trap, maybe we can turn the tables on them. Where is this tomb?"

Wyn sighs. "I'll take you there, Nixy, but promise me, we go together. There's no way you're going anywhere alone anymore. Not after the Black."

"Fine," I say to him, then I think to myself, *You're ready. You're ready for this, Nix.*

Maybe I'm a bald-faced liar. But there's no time to figure it out. Not now.

Wyn asks for my hand, and I pull him upright. "Let's go, then."

Walking in a cemetery in the middle of the night probably appeals to the same kind of people who watch horror movies for fun. I'm not one of those people. It's dark and creepy, and every time the beam from Wyn's flashlight lands on the face of a sculpted angel, I nearly jump out of my skin. But I'm determined not to show fear anymore. I want the old Nixy back, and I want her now.

"Are you sure you know which one?" I ask him for the twelfth time. "Lotta tombs here, you know. Wouldn't want to wake the dead."

All the way over here, first in Larry's loving grip, then on the motorcycle, Wyn and I have tried to keep the tone light. That "go alone" part of the message was a good indication that this next part may not be a dance at the Tropicana. But neither one of us wants to dwell on it, at least not until we have to.

"The Nuñez Galvez tomb is the only one I've actually completed that has a working door." He waves a hand at all the mausoleums and statues we're passing. "The rest of these are just shells."

"So what's inside the Noonie Galvin tomb?" I say, enjoying the look Wyn gives me as I completely mangle the name.

"Trained attack monkeys? No, no, you've done those before. I've got it, you keep Larry's playmates in there. Pet tarantulas named Curly and Moe?"

Wyn laughs. "You're close. Ghosts, and their names are José and Lola."

Now I'm laughing too. "And do they like to play banana fetch or do they have more ghoulish pastimes?"

"Well, Lola likes to recite poetry and José plays chess."

"Classy," I say. "Are they—were they—real people once like Hemingway and Josephine?"

Wyn nods. "Yep, Lola Rodríguez de Tío and José Martí. Cuban heroes. Both of them are buried in the real Colon Cemetery. Mama Beti used to visit their graves when she was a girl, so I thought it would be fun to re-create them for her."

"Well, just make sure you warn her first. Mama Beti's been through enough. The last thing she needs is that kind of a surprise, no matter how civilized José and Lola are."

"Will do," Wyn says, then points his flashlight at the structure ahead.

"Why did we do this at night?" I wonder aloud. "Can't you hit the lights in here? Make it, like, noon or something?"

Wyn shakes his head. "I only built that functionality into the island. Here we are."

While all the other tombs look gothic and old-fashioned, almost like miniature churches, the Nuñez Galvez one looks sleek and triangular, like an open tent—only it's huge and made of stone.

"We should make s'mores," I say, as we approach. "I bet Lola and José would love them."

"We'll have to come back one day and picnic with them," Wyn agrees.

"Once I get out of here," I tell him, "I am never, ever coming back."

As we get closer, I see that the gaping triangular opening leads to a staircase descending into the earth. There's a door at the bottom, and Wyn trains the flashlight on it. "Ready?" he asks.

I nod and look around. "Nobody around with shovels, are there?" I say, remembering his nightmare of being buried alive.

Wyn shudders and we're both silent for a moment.

"All right, let's do this," I say as we begin our descent down the steps.

We walk slowly, both of us hoping beyond hope to find one thing behind that door: a big, sparkly virtual mall.

Wyn undoes the latch and I push open the door.

Darkness.

Black.

I brace myself, fight the urge to run.

Wyn aims the flashlight inside.

But it's only darkness.

There's no Black here.

No nothingness.

I can handle it.

I *will* handle it.

"Lola? José?" Wyn calls, as we step into the shadows. "It's not usually so dark in here," he explains, waving his flashlight around.

SLAM.

The door behind us shuts, and Wyn drops the flashlight.

We are bathed in pitch darkness, except for the weak beam of light at our feet.

"Inventory!" I yell automatically, but it's too late.

The zombies get us first.

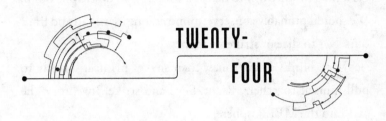

TWENTY-FOUR

WE WAKE UP BACK INSIDE THE TENT-LIKE TOMB AT THE TOP OF THE stairs. Wyn and I stare at each other for a moment.

"I don't know whether to be excited or terrified," he says.

"Same here. Someone's tampered with your tomb, which means it *could* be some kind of portal like the message said, only..."

"Only it's guarded by the undead."

I start twirling a strand of hair around my finger, untwirling it, then twirling it again. I briefly consider that this is not the most mature habit, but it helps me think and we need a plan.

Wyn still looks a bit dazed from the zombie attack. I don't blame him. No one likes having their intestines ripped out. At least they killed us fast.

"Okay," I say, taking charge. I've dealt with zombies in my mini-games with Chang and Moose. "We need to go through our inventories again and divvy up the weapons before we go back in. The only way to defeat a zombie is to destroy its brain. We should probably conserve ammo as long as we can and limit ourselves to slice or strike weaponry."

Wyn blinks a few times, then shakes his head briskly to pull himself together. "Right. Slice and strike. Inventory," he says into the MEEPosphere.

"How about a crowbar?" he asks, after a few seconds of perusing.

"Perfect," I answer. "Let's see, you still have the Gladius sword and laser guns I gave you earlier, right?"

He nods. "Laser guns are both on low power, though. What about the grenades? I still have five left. Why not toss them in and get rid of the zombies all at once?"

I shake my head. "Too risky. The tomb might cave in and destroy the portal. Or we could break the code, like I did in Mama Beti's room, and then . . ."

Wyn blows out a breath. "Right, say no more. No grenades. What have you got?"

"Rappelling gun, crossbow, machete, and a shield. Half a quiver left for the bow. And a potato gun."

Wyn raises an eyebrow at me. "In case we get hungry?"

I grimace. "Long story."

"I'll trade you my brass knuckles for the potato gun," he says, like we're in kindergarten.

"You're on," I say, "but you gotta throw in half a tuna sandwich to seal the deal."

"Only if you give me the creamy half of your Oreo."

"You're a tough negotiator, Elwyn Brooks Salvador," I say, as we trade weapons. "So what are you doing with brass knuckles anyway?"

Wyn looks at me mysteriously. "Oh, you know, Havana in the 1950s can be a dangerous place . . . mobsters, shady politicians, money lenders . . . you never know when you might get caught in a brawl." He's grinning now, and I can't tell if he's teasing me or not.

"You programmed your Meeple to get in fistfights?" I ask.

He laughs. "Nah, it's just one of my extras, when I want a break from building. I put in a boxing ring inside a bar called Sloppy Joe's. Most of my opponents are Meeple, but I also have a rock golem and a robozilla in the rotation. They're a little tougher to crack."

"I am seriously sorry I didn't get to see one of your matches," I say, and I mean it. I would love to see Wyn take on a rock golem. "You ever win?"

Wyn shrugs. "What do you think?"

"I'll reserve judgment until after we take out the zombies," I reply.

"Speaking of zombies . . . shall we, señorita?" he says, extending his elbow to me in gentlemanly fashion.

I give him a little curtsy and slip my hand around his arm. "By all means, kind sir. I believe it is time to kick some undead fanny."

We head down the stairs and pause for a second before the door.

"Three, two, one," I say, and Wyn kicks it open.

As previously agreed, he goes left, I go right, and we both start swinging. The zombies on the left get treated to a head-bashing by crowbar; the zombies on the right suffer full or partial decapitation by my machete. I've equipped myself with the night-vision goggles, though I almost wish I didn't have to see what I'm doing. The whole thing's pretty gross. Close combat has never been my cup of tea, but I keep hacking away, my machete doing its thing.

Wyn has strapped the flashlight to his left arm, which he tries to keep raised so he can see what's coming, but given that he's also fending off a mob of flesh-hungry monsters, the lighting for him is erratic at best. We both count aloud every time we score a hit so we can get a sense of how many enemies we're dealing with—especially important if we're defeated and have to do this Zombie Cha-Cha all over again.

"Eight!" yells Wyn. He's just caught up to me. I better step up my game.

I start spinning a 360, my machete raised at neck level. *THUNK THUNK THUNK*, I hear as my weapon makes contact. "Nine, ten, eleven!" I yell. Fortunately, the zombies disappear as soon as we kill them, otherwise we'd be tripping over the body pile. I swing some more and get nothing but air.

"All clear on the right!" I holler at Wyn.

Wyn raises his flashlight arm and finds me in his beam. "All clear here, too," he says. "How many was that total? Nineteen?"

"Nineteen? We're missing one," I say, looking around and keeping my machete up.

Wyn sidles around in the dark, his crowbar at the ready, his flashlight arm up and pointed. He reminds me of Buzz Lightyear. "How do you know we're missing one?" he asks.

"Who creates an army of nineteen zombies? It's too . . . prime."

"Too prime?" Wyn says, and I hear the amusement in his voice. Then I see the shadow behind him.

"Get down!" I yell.

He drops to his knees just as my machete swings through the space his head occupied a second ago. *THUNK.*

"Twelve," I say, offering a hand to Wyn as he gets back to his feet. "For a total of twenty."

"Nice even numbers," he says, nodding at me in mock admiration. "You must be well pleased."

I'm about to remind him that my insistence on even numbers just kept his brains from being some zombie's Snack Pack pudding, but the lights go on, nearly blinding us.

I blink my eyes shut, then open them. Everything is white. Oh God, not the maze from hell again. Please no.

"Inventory!" I yell, bracing myself.

But then I see that everything is white because it is snowing. And it is snowing because it is Christmas in the Landing. I twirl around and see Wyn's face transform from wariness to relief as he slowly comes to the same realization.

"Oh my God. We did it, Nixy!" he says, his voice loud with excitement. "Hot damn. We're home!" he yells, then picks me up and starts spinning me around in the snow.

We're both laughing now, giddy with relief and happiness, or maybe it's pure exhaustion, I don't know. But we gaze into each other's eyes and smile and laugh and twirl in that big virtual mall like we've just found a pot of gold at the end of the rainbow. A Meeple choir sings, "Have a holly jolly Christmas" in the background, though a strange whirring noise interrupts.

We look up from our celebratory hugfest and see a cute animatronic penguin on wheels rolling toward us. In his flippers, he's holding a gift-wrapped present with a tag that reads To WYN, FROM SANTA.

Wyn looks at me with an expression of surprised

amusement. "One of your dad's ideas?"

"Must be . . ." I start to say, though something's nagging at me. "Wait—"

I'm too late.

Wyn opens the box and we explode.

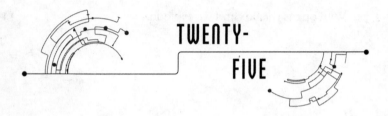

TWENTY-FIVE

AS SOON AS MY EYES OPEN, I SCRAMBLE UP, INVENTORY AT THE READY.

Wyn jumps to his feet next to me. We're still in the Landing, right where we last fell.

Why? *Why?* my brain screams. Why the explosion if not to send us back a level to the cemetery?

"Beware penguins bearing false gifts," I joke, but neither one of us is in the mood for humor now. I'm already scanning for the next challenge that awaits us, and so is Wyn. He's got both laser guns out and is doing a slow sweep of the mall.

The Landing is deathly quiet now and it has stopped snowing. The Meeple choir has vanished. There are no festively dressed shoppers roaming, no elves passing out discount flyers, no mini-games in action. Just twinkling lights everywhere and, in the middle of the atrium, the big three-story Christmas tree opposite the Information Desk.

The beautiful Information Desk.

That big, shiny, blinking control panel on top of it is all I need to shut this game down.

And it's only a pool's length away. . . .

An Olympic-size pool, but still. It's doable.

I just have to get there without dying.

My legs are ready, poised for a mad dash to the desk.

I will myself to be still.

Focus, I think. Just like chess.

Study the board.

Anticipate your opponent.

Think before you move.

Focus.

"See anything?" I ask Wyn.

"Nothing," he says. "But I don't like this. It's too quiet."

Somewhere nearby we hear a tiny *tinkling* sound and we both jump.

A pretty red-and-silver Christmas ornament rolls toward us.

Wyn doesn't waste any time. He shoots it.

The ornament explodes into a thousand little pieces and . . . that's it. It was just an ornament.

Wyn swears under his breath. "Someone's messing with us, Nixy. They're watching, I can feel it."

I feel it too, but I don't want to believe it. We're too damn close to home. "All we have to do is get to the main controls. Hit the Reset button. That should automatically boot us out," I say, remembering my dad's conversation with Diego Salvador.

Wyn raises his eyebrows at me. "In theory, you mean."

"In theory," I concede. "And Wyn—"

"I know," he says.

I say it anyway. I have to. "It will destroy everything you've built here—the Floridita, Mama Beti's house, Larry, the treehouse—it will all disappear in a blink."

Wyn nods, his face resigned. "Understood. Let's get it over with."

"Okay. Slowly."

He nods and we sniper-walk toward the desk.

Step, step, step. We gain a few feet.

We pass by Medieval Moderne, the boutique where I bought my wench dress, and I do a double take. The mannequin in the window is wearing the very same meadow-green dress as mine, but that's not what catches my eye. The mannequin is actually a skeleton . . . a skeleton who's accessorized the dress with a jaunty sailor cap. And it looks like she's smiling at me.

CLICK CLICK go her jaws, then all hell breaks loose.

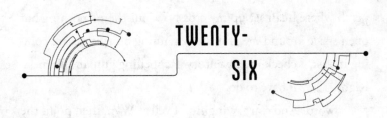

TWENTY-SIX

THE SKELETON HORDE RUSHES US FROM ALL SIDES. ALL THE mannequins in the mall have been transformed into a walking, stalking army of bones.

"Laser gun and grenades!" I bark at Wyn, pulling out my machete and oak shield. I'd prefer to use my crossbow, but it will be useless at close range; I need to find an eagle's nest and *fast*.

Within seconds Wyn picks off the leaders of the pack with the laser guns, then lobs the grenades in quick succession. They explode in a perfect circle around us—one, two, three, four, five. Once the pile of bones and boas, bathrobes, and boots disappears, I quickly assess the damage. Looks like my fighting partner just halved our enemy.

"Nice!" I yell to Wyn, who's already back on laser gun duty.

"These guns aren't gonna last much longer," he yells back. As if to prove his point, both lasers die on cue.

Damn. I look around again, desperate to find a protected perch where I can set up my crossbow, but there's nothing but open space around me and the remaining boneheads are coming in fast. I check my inventory. Rappelling gun and harness. Right. They'll have to do.

"Sword! And start swinging," I yell at Wyn, then point the rappelling gun straight up.

Whoosh. Thwack! The grappling hook lodges in the ceiling three stories above me and whips me into the air above the fray. I dangle there, like the angel from a Christmas play, only instead of a harp I have a loaded crossbow.

Forty arrows left and I need to make each one count. The skeletons have begun to close in on Wyn, forming a circle around him. He's got the Gladius sword out and he's crouched and ready in the middle, looking around wildly.

"Nixy, where are you?" he shouts.

"Up here!" I yell back, then I get to work. I start with the inner circle of skeletons, twirling on my hook like a jewelry box ballerina. Only five shots later I'm in the zone, working the crossbow on automatic pilot. The boneheads are momentarily confused as their comrades go down one by one, but then my buddy Sailor Cap spots me overhead.

Uh-oh.

I've managed to pick off about twenty so far, but there are still nearly that many left and now they're coming after *me*.

Four of them drop their weapons and form the base of a cheerleading tower underneath me. Four more climb up on their shoulders. I shoot two of them, but two more hop on faster than I can reload. Now they're three skeletons high and I have to reel myself higher. When I spy Sailor Cap stick his saber between his jaws and start climbing, I know I need a new plan of action.

I look down at Wyn, who's fending off two skeletons, the only two who haven't joined the cheerleaders. Though I respect their decision to distance themselves from the rah-rahs, I shoot them anyway. Wyn looks up at me.

"Take out the tower!" I yell. "Hurry!"

He pauses for a second, baffled by the bonehead acrobatics.

"Cut 'em down at the knees!" I yell, and he springs into action.

The tower wobbles this way and that as Wyn hacks at the femurs below. Every time one bonehead goes down, the others rebuild just as fast. I pump my legs like a gymnast to propel myself away from them and try to keep the ones on top from grabbing my feet. Sailor Cap is now standing on top of the column like a pirate, brandishing his saber at me. I try to aim the crossbow at him, but it's no use; we're all teetering around like drunken hobos. I've only got two arrows left and I don't want to waste them on wild shots. Instead, I channel the playground, and swing for him with everything I've got. Combat boots first, I make contact with his skull and knock Sailor Cap to the floor below.

Feels good, but it's a temporary fix.

The dwindling boneheads get smart now and regroup. There are only eight of them left. Three peel off to gang up on Wyn. That leaves five for me, and they quickly form a skeletal ladder underneath me. My BFF, Sailor Cap, begins to scramble up to the top again. He's ripped the skirt and apron off his dress, so he's just wearing the bodice now, which somehow looks obscene. I quickly load my crossbow and take aim, but below me a bonehead lands his axe in Wyn's thigh. Wyn falls to the ground.

Crap.

Wyn manages to lop off the head of the offending skeleton with the Gladius sword, but he's still got two more coming in. I shoot my crossbow downward and quickly pick them off, one after the other. Wyn turns his head up and starts to smile at me, but his face registers instant alarm.

"Behind you!" he yells.

I spin around and find myself eye socket–to–eye socket with Sailor Cap. He raises his saber to strike, but I fling my crossbow at him, hoping to knock him off the tower. He drops his saber and sways left and right, swinging his bony arms in frantic circles for balance. Which he achieves.

CLICK CLICK sound his teeth, and the skeleton on the bottom passes up a hatchet he's got stashed in his leg warmers.

I am *so* not in the mood for an axe to the head.

"Think think think!" I order myself.

Sailor Cap reaches out an arm and tries to snatch me from my hook.

An arm. That's it. I lunge toward him and grab *his* arm, pulling as hard as I can.

"Learned that trick from you, pal," I say as the entire arm shaft comes out of his shoulder socket.

Sailor Cap now has the hatchet in his hand, the one still attached to him, but I don't give him a chance to raise it. I swing that dismembered bony arm with both hands and knock his skull right off its block.

"Home run, baby!" cheers Wyn below, still struggling to get to his feet on his injured leg.

I wave my bony bat in victory, then quickly access my inventory. I've still got four skeletons left but now I'm on a roll. I grab the machete, then click the switch on my harness to release the line. As I come barreling down the rappelling rope, I slice right through the skeleton tower, counting as I go. "Four, three, two, one!" I holler, landing on my feet with a flourish.

I release the harness, drop the machete, and run over to Wyn.

"Are you okay?" I ask, kneeling beside him.

"You are amazing," he answers, and I try not to look too pleased by this.

"I asked how *you* were," I say. "Do you think you can walk?"

Wyn shakes his head. "Whole right leg is totally worthless. Just leave me here and go press that damn Reset button before something else happens."

He's right, of course, but still I hesitate to leave him.

He reaches both his hands up now and takes my face between them. "I'll see you on the other side," he says, then pulls me in for a kiss. It's a short kiss, more like a peck, really, but it still takes my virtual breath away.

All of a sudden it rushes back to me. Wyn . . . the top of the hotel.

"Now go!" he yells, breaking into my memories.

"Right," I say, hopping to my feet.

As I run for the Information Desk, two things happen.

One, Rico Suave appears.

Two, I see that he has a minotaur.

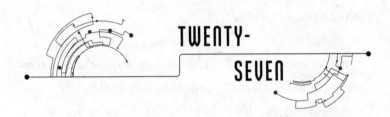

TWENTY-SEVEN

I DON'T BELIEVE THIS.

"Guard the hostage," Rico Suave orders the minotaur. "I'll take care of this one."

This one? I think. I am a ball of fury at this point. Because I *know* there's a human brain behind Rico Suave, a real person keeping us imprisoned here, putting us through death by zombies and skeletons and exploding penguins....

Not to mention the Black, for God's sake.

He has been mentally torturing us. I want to kill him.

"Inventory!" I yell, though I've got nothing left but an oak shield and a pair of brass knuckles. Oh well. Sometimes you have to make do. I equip myself with the knuckles and charge.

My sudden offensive takes Rico Suave by surprise. A brassy

right hook to the jaw takes him in a flash down to the floor, where I pin him with my knees, just like I did to Kora.

"Who are you?" I yell at him. "Why are you doing this?"

Rico opens his mouth to answer. "Inventory! Strength potion! Samurai kanabo!"

Damn.

Before I even know what's happening, he uses the potion to shake me off like a flea and jumps to his feet. He brandishes the kanabo—a long wooden club fortified with iron spikes around the end—and puts himself between me and the Information Desk.

"Initiate your frequency code," Rico Suave orders me.

"What? Now you *want* us to leave?" I say, my mind whirling, trying to make sense of things.

"You. The code. Now."

"The code doesn't work. And anyway, I'm not leaving without him," I say, looking over at Wyn. He's still lying on the floor, glaring at Rico's new sidekick, who, though much less attractive than Josephine/Kora, looks a whole lot deadlier. The man-bull looms over Wyn like an overgrown guard dog, his enormous bull head right in Wyn's face, his flared nostrils steaming.

"It will work now," Rico says, spinning the kanabo in his hands like a baton, "and you *will* initiate it."

If there's one thing I don't like, it's some Rico Suave bossing me around.

"Look, *rasshøl*, I said I'm not leaving without him and I meant it." I turn my head again to make sure the minotaur's not hurting Wyn, but both of them are now faced in our direction, listening to the conversation. Wyn looks just as baffled as I am and almost as mad.

"Do what he says, Nixy," Wyn calls. "Go. I'll be fine."

"No," I yell behind my shoulder. "We leave together."

Rico Suave starts to chuckle, but the laugh sounds more bitter than amused. "Only six days together and you're ready to die for this guy, Nixy? Six days and you turn into a lovestruck stooge? That must have been a really great kiss back there. Or maybe, maybe it was all your time together on the island. . . ."

I open my mouth to reply, but nothing comes out. While one part of my brain puts the puzzle pieces together, another part resists the solution. The MEEP Mail, the kanabo . . . the jealousy?

I can't deny it any longer. My anger turns to grief. I walk slowly toward Rico Suave, who watches me warily, weapon raised.

"I want to see the real you," I say quietly in his direction.

Evan Chan-Gonzalez appears before me. My friend. My enemy? I want to cry.

"Why?" I say, my voice breaking. "What are you doing here? And why?"

Chang's face is stony, emotionless. "I told you to stay home,

Nixy. None of this is your concern. Walk away. I'll give you one last chance."

"One last chance? This isn't a game, Chang. Wyn's been in here for days, his body's back home stuck with tubes and wires. And Kora . . . what happened to Kora? Is she . . . ?"

The minotaur roars.

Chang's face darkens. "Sometimes sacrifices must be made for the greater good. And if you want to blame someone, try Diego Salvador. He could have shut down the MEEP at any time, and he didn't. He chose profit over his own son."

"That's not true! He just didn't want anyone to get hurt."

Chang shakes his head with mock pity in his eyes. "Diego Salvador lied to you, Nixy. He doesn't care about you or me or even his own kid. He could have ended this days ago if he'd just met our demands and shut down the MEEP."

"What demands?"

"The Legionnaires sent him a ransom note a week ago, before Salvador called you in."

I open my mouth to reply, but I'm not sure how. Chang's word against Diego Salvador's? I don't trust either of them at this point. I glance at Wyn, but he's staring at Chang, his jaw set.

"Salvador's nothing but a megalomaniac, intent on controlling the world, one foolish player at a time," Chang continues. "LEGION tried to force his hand, to show him how dangerous the MEEP could be. We thought once we put his only son in harm's way, he'd back down, negotiate with us. But even that didn't stop him. The only thing he cares about is his multibillion-dollar investment."

"Even if you're right, Chang, and I'm not saying you are . . . you have to stop this!"

"Of course I'm right! You *know* I am. Look how the MEEP can be used against people—to manipulate them, torture them, fracture their memories, maybe permanently. Once we're all on MEEP frequencies, what's to stop Diego Salvador and his allies from keeping us completely under their control? They're using us like lab rats, Nix. I've been trying to tell you this for months, but you never pay attention. All you care about is yourself, your dumb college plans, whatever's best for you. But there's a whole world out there, Nixy, and it's in danger. I *can't* stop. Because Diego Salvador's got to be stopped."

His words make me feel ill. He's right in more ways than one. I have been self-absorbed; I haven't been listening to him. And he's right about the MEEP. During the past six days I've experienced the worst this virtual world has to offer. But I've also seen the best of it. Diego Salvador may be a liar, but Wyn's not to blame for that. Wyn doesn't deserve to be a pawn in this game.

"I'm sorry, Chang. But you're no better than your enemies when you resort to blackmail and kidnapping," I finally say.

"Innocent people are getting hurt."

Chang frowns. "Like him?" he scoffs, pointing to Wyn. "The heir to the Salvador fortune? Don't assume he's any better than his father, or you're bound to be disappointed. In any case, we can't let him go home now. Salvador can't hide his son's disappearance forever. Word will get out; people will demand answers. MeaParadisus will be shut down by any means necessary. Get out now, while you still have the chance. Let Wyn pay the piper for his father's greed."

I can't believe what I'm hearing. My oldest friend has just condemned Wyn to a lifelong coma in the real world. No matter how much good he thinks he's doing, how could Chang be so heartless, so arrogant? Anger overtakes me.

"Why don't *you* pay the piper, Chang?" I yell, launching myself at the kanabo. I front-kick Chang in the stomach and he drops his weapon. I grab the kanabo and swing it above my head, determined to take Chang down at the knees.

"Inventory! Laser gun!" he yells, and points the gun at my head.

Fy fæn. He's pulled an Indiana Jones on me.

"Listen to me," Chang says, his voice like cold steel. "If I shoot, you'll die and wake up to another skeleton horde. You don't have the strength or the supplies to defeat them again. You know that. They'll kill you in minutes, and then you'll wake up all over again to another attack. You'll be stuck here in an endless loop along with your . . . friend," he says, glancing disdainfully at Wyn. "We tried to warn you, Nixy. Now initiate the code or die."

I feel dizzy. The whole world is spinning around me like some bad carnival ride. I take a step backward, trying to make the nausea go away. How could Chang do this to me? How could he betray me like this? And Moose . . . did he know about this?

We tried to warn you, Nixy, Chang had said.

We?

The minotaur is roaring again and Chang gives him a look of annoyance.

Suddenly I understand.

"Moose!" I yell at the minotaur.

The minotaur stops roaring and looks at me.

It's him.

"I know you don't want to do this! People are getting hurt . . . Kora may even be dead. Moose, this isn't you!"

The minotaur hesitates.

"Stay in line, Moose!" Chang orders, waving the laser gun at him.

Uh-oh. That's all it takes. Moose charges.

Not at me, not at Wyn . . . Moose charges at Chang.

Chang aims the laser gun at Moose and shoots.

No no no, my mind is screaming, but Moose does not fall.

Chang has misfired. Something has hit him right in the stomach.

A potato.

I look over and see Wyn firing the potato gun from the floor like Billy the Kid.

"Run!" Wyn yells.

Right. He means me. My brain engages my legs and I make a mad dash for the Information Desk.

I'm a few feet away when I hear Wyn cry, "No!"

Moose roars in agony or rage, I can't say.

What's happening behind me?

For a fleeting second, I pause.

It's enough for Chang. I feel the laser beam hit between my shoulder blades.

Don't die, don't die, don't die.

Everything starts to go blurry, but I can still see the blinking yellow RESET button straight ahead.

I make one last lunge for the control panel.

And then . . . nothing.

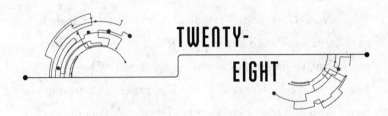

TWENTY-
EIGHT

THE BEEPING IN MY EAR IS GETTING LOUDER, BUT I PUSH IT AWAY.
I need to keep sleeping, dreaming. These dreams are important
somehow, but the beeping has made them scurry off like frightened cats. I try to coax them back, searching the corners of my
brain carefully, gently, so as not to startle them again.

"Nixy? Nixy, can you hear me?" a voice says.

The dreams scatter, fleeing to dark shadows.

"Nixy, it's Dad. Can you hear me?"

Dad. My brain knows that voice, that person.

The dreams pounce all at once, like they've caught a rat.
Everything comes back to me in a sudden rush—the MEEP,
Havana, Chang, Moose, Wyn.

Wyn.

I sit up straight and a sharp pain in my arm makes me gasp. I'm on the hospital bed, covered in tubes and wires. An IV is attached to my arm with a needle, which I've nearly ripped out in my haste.

"Whoa, Nixy, relax," says Dad, who looks extremely haggard, but also relieved and happy. "It's okay now, you're back."

I want to hug him, but there's no time. "Where's Wyn?" I say, trying to look over at his bed, but there's a crowd in the way. Diego Salvador, two doctors in scrubs, Mama Beti in her chair—all have their backs to me, hovering over Wyn's bedside in between medical carts and monitors.

"What's wrong with him, Dad, is he okay?"

Dad tries to give me a reassuring smile. "I'm sure he'll be fine. He's just starting to wake up . . . you both came out of the MEEP at the same time, but it's taking him a little longer to recover. He was in there longer than you so the adjustment's bound to be a little tougher for him."

Thank God. Wyn made it home.

"Listen, Dad, I need you to call home, call Police Chief Cuparino. Tell him he needs to locate Chang as soon as possible and keep him in custody."

Dad looks at me like I'm crazy. "Chang?"

"Dad, just do it. We don't have much time."

Dad still looks dazed. "Nix, the police can't just lock someone up—a minor, no less—because we ask them to."

"Then tell him Chang might be an accessory to murder. Maybe even a murderer himself for all I know. Tell him they also need to find Moose and make sure he's okay."

"Nixy—"

"Dad! Trust me, please. I'll explain everything later."

Dad leans down and kisses me on the forehead. "Okay, Nix, I'll do it. But you need to lie back down and rest. Your mom should be here any minute. She was going frantic at home so she finally packed up Hodee and hopped in the car yesterday. She's been driving nonstop."

"It'll be good to see them," I say, and smile to show my thanks. I see him take out his cell phone and walk into the hallway.

I gulp down the huge glass of water on the table next to me, then grab on to my IV pole and drag it through the crowd around Wyn's bed. Wyn is still sleeping, but I can see eye movement behind his lids. The doctors ignore me. Mama Beti gives me a small smile, then turns her attention back to Wyn. Diego Salvador frowns at me.

"What happened? You've been gone for days," he says, his voice filled with accusation.

"There were *complications*," I say, matching his tone. "Where's Kora?"

Salvador narrows his eyes at me. "What do you know about Kora?"

"Where is she?" I ask, not caring that everyone else, the doctors and Mama Beti, all look up at me in surprise. I don't suppose they've ever heard anyone challenge Diego Salvador before. Least of all a teenage girl.

Salvador hesitates and eyes me like I'm some kind of vermin, spoiling his property. "We don't know," he says in a clipped voice. "She hasn't arrived for work for the past five days, nor has she called to explain her absence. How—"

Wyn's eyes flutter open then, saving me from further interrogation. He looks confused. I know the feeling.

"Wyn!" his father says, rather loudly. "Wyn, are you okay?"

"Shhh," Mama Beti says, gently stroking Wyn's arm.

Wyn blinks several times, then takes a moment to look around at everybody. "Nixy," he says, when his eyes land on me. His voice is raspy, scratchy, not more than a whisper.

"Water!" Diego Salvador demands, and one of the doctors holds a glass of water to Wyn's lips.

Mama Beti squeezes Wyn's hand and says, "Slowly, *mi amor.*" He squeezes her hand in return and gives her a weak yet warm smile.

"Thank God you're home safe, son," Diego Salvador says, laying a hand on Wyn's head.

Wyn gives his father a nod, but the warmth has left his face.

So I'm not the only one left cold by Chang's story.

Wyn's eyes return to me. Then he pulls on Mama Beti's

hand and she leans forward. Wyn whispers something in her ear.

Mama Beti nods, then rises on her walker. "Everybody out!" she says.

Nobody moves.

"I say OUT! *Vamanos!*" she yells again. "We give the boy five minutes to himself."

"Mother—" begins Diego Salvador, but Mama Beti shoots him a look.

I love this woman.

"Go go go," Mama Beti insists, gripping her walker like she might hit someone with it.

The doctors look at Salvador, who blows out a frustrated breath, then nods. "Five minutes," he says to Wyn, then follows the others out the door.

I still haven't moved.

"Nixy, come here," Mama Beti orders, and I do what she says. Together we walk slowly toward the door. When we get there, she reaches out a hand and runs it gently down my cheek. "*Gracias, linda.* You saved my *amorcito.* Thank you."

I reach over her walker and hug her with my one free arm. I can't help it. She smiles and hugs me back.

"Now go to him," she says. "Five minutes."

Wyn is trying to free himself from the tubes and wires, but he is weak, and even more entangled with tubes than I am.

"Help me with these," he says, struggling to remove them.

"Better stay hooked up for now," I say, perching on the side of his bed, careful not to jostle anything. "You need to get your strength back. You know they're going to ask us a thousand and one questions soon."

As if on cue, Dad sticks his head in the door. "Nix?"

I can't believe he got past Mama Beti.

"Sorry to interrupt, but I thought you'd want to know that Moose is safe and sound. His mom says he's shaken up about something but refuses to talk about it. Chief Cuparino hasn't located Chang yet, but he's got several men looking for him."

I sigh in relief and the knots in my stomach loosen. Moose is okay. That's all I care about right now. I hear Mama Beti scolding Dad in the background and he gives me a quick wink, then closes the door.

"Good news about Moose," Wyn says, his voice still raspy. "Any word on Kora?"

I shake my head and pass him the glass of water. "Your father says she's gone missing." I pause and look out the window at the blue ocean. "I'm glad we made it out, Wyn, but there are still so many unanswered questions, so much we don't know. . . ."

Wyn closes his eyes for a moment, as if the thought has pained him. "I know. I'm not sure I can bear to think about it right now."

"Then don't," I say. "I'll get Mama Beti to keep the wolves at bay for as long as you need."

Wyn smiles at me then, and those chocolate eyes make my stomach cartwheel. "You're even prettier in real life, you know," he says, reaching up a hand to tug gently on my hair.

"You're just delirious after all that MEEP sleep," I tease, though I lean forward to run my fingers down his cheek. His skin feels warm and soft under my fingers . . . alive. I place my hand on his chest and feel the steady beat of his heart. We are home.

"One more thing before they come back," I say.

"What's that?" he whispers, almost breathless. He pulls me down farther.

The human Wyn, the true flesh-and-blood Wyn, is making my palms sweat, my skin tingle, and my heart do jumping jacks. I've never felt happier to be in my own body, even if it gives me away.

"I remember," I tell him.

He stares into my eyes, his expression full of relief. "I didn't think you'd ever—"

"I do," I say.

"Then what are you waiting for?"

I pause. "For real?" I ask.

"For real," he says.

And so I kiss him.

I really do.

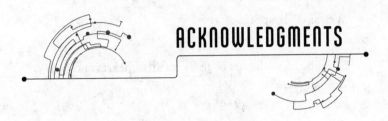

ACKNOWLEDGMENTS

I could not have finished the game without my family and friends, who fed me, encouraged me, and kicked me in the pants whenever I needed to level up. Extra thanks to the following people who went above and beyond every time I asked for help, and even when I didn't.

Kristen "Plot Babe" Pettit

Tracey & Josh "Ninja Agents" Adams

Samantha "Girl Got Game" Bagood

Kyle "Híjole" Durango

Tracie "Peaches" Vaughn Zimmer

Abbie "Bada$$" Zimmer

Linda Sue "Scarecrow" Park

Bill "The River Keep" Cairns

Susie "Eagle Eye" Stephenson
Larry & Susan "Los Padres" Greider
&
of course, the entire
Westside "Best Side" Crew

May your health bars be forever full of hearts and your coffers full of booty.

Read on for a sneak peek of

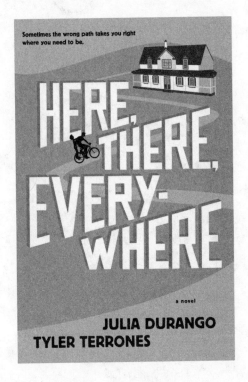

Sometimes the wrong path takes you right
where you need to be.

HERE, THERE, EVERY- WHERE

a novel

JULIA DURANGO
TYLER TERRONES

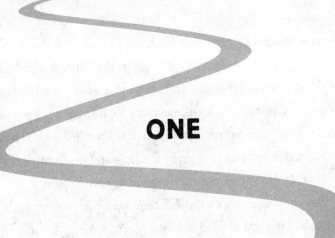

ONE

WE'VE ALL HAD THAT ONE DREAM.

No, not the one where your teeth crumble and fall out of your head, and you desperately try to catch the falling shards of bicuspids, incisors, and shattered molars in your hands, to no avail.

Not the one where you can fly or where you wake up right before you hit the ground. Those are kind of exciting.

And no, not *that* one either. My head isn't that far in the gutter.

I'm talking about the other one. The one where you're suddenly in school wearing nothing but your underwear. Where the hell are your pants? And why the hell is no one noticing?

That dream.

I've had it regularly since kindergarten, and it's never any fun. I don't even wear underwear in real life. I mean, I don't go *commando*—I wear boxer briefs, to be specific—but why am I always wearing the damn tightie-whities in that dream?

You know the only good part about that dream, though? It's the enormous relief you feel when you wake up and consciousness washes over you like a warm, soothing wave. Even as you stumble into your mundane, everyday life filled with alarm clocks, midterms, and your crazy family—and my family's crazier than most, believe me—at least you're wearing pants.

But pants or no pants, those dreams were nothing compared to how bad my real life had been going.

It had been exactly forty-seven days since Mom had uprooted me and my little brother, Grub, from our lifelong home in Chicago and transplanted us a hundred miles west to the small town of Buffalo Falls, aka Nowhere, Illinois.

Seriously, it's *small*. Like, one high school, two supermarkets, three burger joints, six churches, and eight bars small. Plus, one brand-spanking-new vegetarian café, owned and operated by none other than my mom, Coriander Gunderson. Free delivery all summer between eleven and two!

That's right, after being the new kids at school one month before summer break, my eight-year-old brother and I had been tasked with the "free delivery" part of my mom's new business venture. Mom insisted Grub needed "fresh air and new scenery" every day and would be a "good little helper." Apparently, she's a little hazy on child labor laws, workers' rights, and occupational safety hazards.

Which is how, the second week of June, I happened to be pedaling across town on her old Schwinn bike with Grub standing on the foot pegs behind me. No waking up from that nightmare.

As always, Grub wore a plastic green army helmet, a camouflage vest over his T-shirt and shorts, and a Nerf bazooka strapped to his back. His little claws dug into my shoulders as I pedaled through town, making salad deliveries.

As we crossed the bridge over the Stone River to the south side of Buffalo Falls, some guy must have noticed our thirst, because he graciously offered us a blue Slurpee out the window of his convertible Jeep Wrangler.

By offered, I mean he winged it at us.

It splattered to our left, spraying cold, sticky sugar water all over our legs. He may have yelled "Losers!" out the window too, but I couldn't hear him over the music playing through my earbuds.

"Fire in the hole!" yelled Grub, which I *did* hear since he was only two inches from my head.

My brother's real name is Manuel (pronounced man-WELL, not MAN-you-el), but I've called him Grub as long as I can remember. I don't know why. He's always looked like a little grub, I guess. A little Puerto Rican–Norwegian grub.

That's right, he's a Puertowegian.

Never heard of a Puertowegian? No surprise. That's probably because one hasn't ever existed in the history of, well, ever.

Except for my World War II–obsessed brother, Manuel Thor Gunderson.

If you think his name is bad, get a load of mine: Jesús Bjorn Gunderson (hey-ZOOS bee-YORN). I know what you're thinking. Another Puertowegian, right?

Wrong.

I have the honor to be Mexiwegian. I think that sounds better than Norwexican. Yep, I'm half Mexican, half Norwegian, like a lutefisk taco. Apparently my mom has a thing for Latin men. Unlike Grub, though, all of my mom's Norwegian features were downloaded into my DNA, so I look more Bjorn than Jesús.

But everyone calls me Zeus.

I'm pretty average looking, I guess. Brown hair, blue eyes, fair skin, 145 pounds. I'm trying to grow sideburns, but so far it looks more like someone glued random hair plugs to my face.

At the moment, though, I was bright red, trying to get the bike ride from hell over as quickly as possible. Grub and I recovered from the Slurpee grenade and made our way up the hill. The director of Hilltop Nursing Home had recently signed up for the 5-Day Deal. It was a coupon special my mom had come up with to attract business to her new shop, the World Peas Café. That day's deal? Make Quinoa, Not War.

I told you my mom was terrible with names.

For the past few weeks, I'd mainly been delivering to downtown business owners, "downtown" referring to the little collection of buildings surrounding a shady park. The nursing home would be our first venture across the bridge to the south side of town.

Following my phone's map app, we turned right at the next stoplight, then a left, then another right into a residential area. The tidy-looking homes on either side of the street provided a stark contrast to the ramshackle houses in our own neighborhood where we rented a ground-level apartment.

Hilltop Nursing Home finally appeared—you guessed it—at the top of the hill, and holy hell, it was huge. Buffalo Falls must have a surplus of old people. And the old-people business must be booming, because this place looked like Buckingham Palace. Not that I'd ever been there, but Jesus (JEE-zus).

A sea of lawn surrounded the castle-like structure.

"Drop-off point at nine o'clock!" Grub yelled in the best army voice an eight-year-old can muster.

You know how I mentioned Grub is obsessed with World War II? That's putting it mildly. Not only had he spent the last few years having Nerf gun fights with his friends in our old Chicago neighborhood, but he could give you a detailed breakdown of the Battle of the Bulge *and* Operation Overlord. By the time he was seven, he'd checked out every volume on World War II history the Chicago Public Library had to offer. He was too young to read them cover to cover, of course, but he loved studying the pictures and maps.

I know, I know, what mother would allow her little boy to

immerse himself in that kind of violence and bloodshed? That would be our peace-loving, antiwar mom, Coriander Gunderson, who also doesn't believe in "shielding her children from hard truths." As long as Grub and I were reading and not staring at a screen, she gave us free rein among the library shelves.

I chained the bike to a bench, and Grub and I headed to the arched entryway of Hilltop Nursing Home. I carried the cardboard salad container—100 percent recycled material, mind you—while Grub dove and tumbled behind me, avoiding imaginary machine gun fire and mortar explosions.

The glass doors opened automatically as we approached, and a wave of nursing-home odor smacked me right in the olfactory receptors.

Now—*disclaimer*—I have nothing against old people. In fact, I hope to be one someday. But we all know that nursing-home odor. It's like if you bottled up the smell of a hospital, added a splash of grade-school cafeteria, then threw in a little diarrhea, and tried to cover it up with Lysol.

Grub commando-crawled past me into the lobby. I heard someone playing the piano in the distance.

Grub ducked beneath a nearby reception desk, Nerf bazooka at the ready. "All clear, Sarge!" he shouted.

Do you know one good thing about nursing homes? Old people love little kids like they love their hard candies. That means it's nearly impossible to be embarrassed by your little brother "playing army," Grub's favorite game.

I approached the lady at the reception desk.

"Hi, are you here to visit someone?" she asked.

"No, actually I'm making a delivery to . . ." I checked the receipt again. "Missy Stouffer."

The woman glanced down at a day planner. "Ms. Stouffer is in a meeting right now, but if you'd like to have a seat in the common room, she'll be with you shortly." She pointed down the hall.

"Thanks," I said, then turned to Grub. "Let's move, Private."

"Sir, yes, sir!" he shouted, barrel-rolling past me to clear the path of enemies.

As we made our way, the piano music got louder and louder. What was that song? It had an old-time, dreamy feel to it. It reminded me of the Beatles for some reason, but I couldn't place it.

The hallway opened up into a large room, where a crowd of white-haired, wrinkly people sat in various armchairs and sofas around a black grand piano, nodding and tapping in time to the music.

As the final chords resonated through the room, the crowd burst into applause, and I glanced over at the piano player. I was expecting some old guy to be sitting there, but I couldn't have been more wrong.

Instead, it was the girl who changed everything.

Also by
JULIA DURANGO

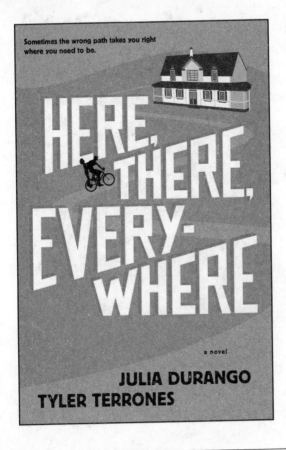

HARPER TEEN
An Imprint of HarperCollins Publishers

JOIN THE

Epic Reads
COMMUNITY

THE ULTIMATE YA DESTINATION

◄ **DISCOVER** ►
your next favorite read

◄ **MEET** ►
new authors to love

◄ **WIN** ►
free books

◄ **SHARE** ►
infographics, playlists, quizzes, and more

◄ **WATCH** ►
the latest videos